CONFLICT
OF INTEREST

Other books by Deborah Nolan:

Suddenly Lily

CONFLICT
OF INTEREST

•

Deborah Nolan

AVALON BOOKS
NEW YORK

Published by Avalon Books,
an imprint of Thomas Bouregy & Co., Inc.
160 Madison Avenue, New York, NY 10016

Library of Congress Cataloging-in-Publication Data

Nolan, Deborah.
    Conflict of interest / Deborah Nolan.
        p. cm.
    ISBN 978-0-8034-7723-0 (alk. paper)
    1. Women lawyers—Fiction.   2. Teenagers—Fiction.
3. Private investigators—Fiction.   4. Organized crime—Fiction.
5. New Jersey—Fiction.   6. Outer Banks (N.C.)—Fiction.
I. Title.

    PS3614.O466C66 2011
    813'.6—dc22

                                            2010037409

PRINTED IN THE UNITED STATES OF AMERICA
ON ACID-FREE PAPER
BY RR DONNELLEY, BLOOMSBURG, PENNSYLVANIA

To my husband and children,
who all continue to inspire me to try harder,
and to my mother, Claire Glennon Madison,
who would be proud, albeit surprised,
to have a writer for a daughter.
I am sorry she missed this chapter.

Acknowledgments

I would like to thank my critique partners Joani Ascher and Kim Zito, who do their best to keep me on track. I also would like to thank members of my former writing group including Freddie Glucksman, Rea Martin, Jane Degnan, Mark Podolski, and Richard Sharpless, who all provided useful insights into various stages of the manuscript. Finally, a special thanks to Mary Elizabeth Allen, whose guidance and editorial comments in an early draft were of great help.

A special thanks to retired New York City lieutenant Christopher Moran for giving me valuable information on the day-to-day workings of the police force. And thank you to the recently retired president of the Port of Newark Container Terminal, Donald Hamm, for sharing his knowledge of the port and surrounding locale. Any mistakes made in either police procedure or port operations are mine. And last, but not least, thanks to Dave Cooke, whose knowledge of Elizabeth was indispensable.

Chapter One

W hen the phone rang, Mary Ellen leaned across the piles
of papers on her desk to answer it. It was 7:30 in the morning.
She was surprised anyone would try to call the office so early.

"Mary Ellen Carey?"

She didn't recognize the male voice, maybe because of the
bad connection.

Before she had a chance to speak, he continued. "You care
about your kids?" he snarled.

"Excuse me?" she managed to stammer. "Who is this?"

"Never mind about that," he said. His voice was harsh,
the New Jersey accent unmistakable.

"Who *is* this?" she repeated, realizing that at this hour she was
probably the only person in the building.

"Just get Anderson off, or else you'll really have something
to worry about," the caller said, before hanging up.

She stared at the receiver. Anderson? He had to mean David
Anderson. She was appearing in court this morning on his
case. It was about a fight he'd had in a local bar; nothing worth

threatening someone's children over. The call had to be a joke, nothing to be taken seriously. Nevertheless, she called home.

"Tim?" she said when her eleven-year-old son answered. "Put Heidi on. I need to speak to her."

"Is everything all right?" asked Mary Ellen when the college girl who looked after her children came on the phone.

"Sure. Everything's fine," said Heidi, clearly puzzled at Mary Ellen's sharp tone.

"I just got a very odd call," Mary Ellen said. "Probably some crackpot making idle threats. I don't have time to go into the details now. Besides, I'm sure it's nonsense and nothing to be concerned about." She was babbling, but was afraid to say anything too specific. "I'd feel better if you would keep the children with you all day."

"Should we stay in the house?"

"No, you don't have to do anything that drastic." She knew her three children, particularly her thirteen-year-old twin daughters, would never tolerate such restrictions without a long explanation—which she wasn't prepared to give, at least not yet.

"Is it still okay to go to the pool?" Heidi asked.

"That's probably the best place to be." Perfect, actually. On a hot day in August anyone who wasn't on vacation or at work would be at the town pool. No one would dare try to harm her children there. And Heidi wouldn't have to explain anything. The three were on the town swim team and had planned to go to the pool anyway.

"You should be fine," Mary Ellen concluded, "but just to be sure, keep the cell phone with you so I can check in later." She would feel much better if she could reach Heidi during the day.

Mary Ellen was still uneasy. Who could it have been? One of David Anderson's friends? They were not an impressive lot. The ones she'd met didn't seem capable of much more than getting drunk and starting fights. If it was one of them, she was worrying over nothing. But the caller had sounded older. Even though it didn't make sense, she dialed the number for the Newark police department.

She knew from her days in the District Attorney's office in Brooklyn that the police would need more than a threatening phone call to take action, but it might make her feel better to report the call. If nothing else, it would establish a record.

"They must be referring to the young man I'm representing on a minor case," she explained to the officer who was taking down the information. "I'm an attorney with Dunphy & Boylan and usually don't handle criminal matters, but David is the son of one of our corporate clients." She hoped that identifying the firm would give her some credibility. Although the law firm was small, with just ten lawyers, it was one of the more respected groups in Newark. But it was obvious from the officer's silence that the name meant nothing to him.

When she got off the phone she still felt uneasy, but now was not the time to dwell on it. It was nearly nine and she needed to meet up with David at the courthouse.

He was waiting for her on the courthouse steps. She'd been toying with the idea of asking him if he knew anything about the call, but the sight of him made her change her mind. Anyone could see that he barely managed to take care of himself. Today was typical. In spite of his court appearance, he had on his usual worn, baggy, dirty jeans and unlaced sneakers. Perhaps as a concession, today he wore a button-down shirt, though it was wrinkled and too small. Although she'd reminded him, he'd forgotten to wear a tie, but she'd anticipated that and brought one of her ex-husband's. It didn't fit her ex's lifestyle anymore, but it might work for David.

As they walked up the steps to the courthouse, she went over the charges with David again. "Remember," she said, observing that his shirt was coming loose from his pants, "if the judge asks you anything, look him in the eye, speak up, and tell the truth."

When he nodded, she handed him the tie. "Now go into the men's room, put this on, and," she added, pointing to his shirt, "pull yourself together and tuck in your shirt. I'll be in the courtroom checking in, so look for me there." She watched as he ambled off, feeling more like his mother than his lawyer.

The courtroom was crowded and there was a low din of muffled voices. After she checked in with the court officer, she walked to the back, looking for seats. She saw two in the last row, and headed over to wait for David. She scanned the courtroom, curious if there was anyone she knew. She recognized few familiar faces, but that wasn't surprising since this wasn't her usual beat.

"Mrs. Carey, what brings you to this neck of the woods?"

"Pardon?" she said, turning in the direction of the voice, wondering who might be addressing her so formally. It was Newark policeman Gerard Fitzpatrick, who was also coaching her son's soccer team. And he was the last person on earth she felt like dealing with this morning. She'd only met him the day before, at Tim's first practice, but it was an encounter she wasn't likely to forget.

Because it was Tim's first time on a sports team, Mary Ellen had been anxious that things go well. She was also concerned because Tim had recently gotten stitches in his leg, and she wanted the coach to know. When they got to the field, Tim had run ahead, mumbling something about telling the coach himself. Mary Ellen had no confidence that he would. Tim was only eleven, and not a very mature eleven at that. She parked the car and walked across the field to speak to Coach Fitzpatrick.

She started to have second thoughts as soon as she came within earshot of the man. Practice had already started, and he didn't even look up to acknowledge her. But she was determined to say her piece. "Excuse me, Mr. Fitzpatrick," she'd said. "Do you think you could possibly spare a moment?" When he didn't answer right away, she could feel her chest tightening in irritation and she took a deep breath. Now was not the time to lose her cool. "Did it occur to you that what I need to speak to you about could be important?" she said, speaking louder.

He swung around to face her. With his chin out and his dark eyes narrowing, he didn't look happy. But even before she saw the expression on his face, she'd begun to wonder if she was coming on too strong, particularly when she looked over at the boys and saw the panicked look on Tim's face. Just thinking about it now made her blush.

Fitzpatrick had walked right up to her then, probably feeling he had no choice if he wanted to avoid a scene. "What's the problem, ma'am?" he'd said, speaking in a solid Jersey accent, his sarcasm matching her own. He brought his face up close to hers and continued. "You're not going to be one of those mothers who's worried about her son not being fairly treated, are you? Or are you planning to be away most weekends and just wanted to warn me that he won't make half the games? What's up? I got a team to coach and time's a wastin'."

"My son, Tim Carey," she explained, speaking very slowly, enunciating carefully, "just had twenty stitches removed from his leg. He insisted on coming to practice. He's afraid you won't keep him on the team if he doesn't. But doctor's orders are that he take it easy."

Before she lost it entirely, she'd quickly turned, ready to stomp off the field. But her heel got stuck in the soft ground and she lost her balance. Automatically, she reached out and grabbed the man to save herself, just as he reached over to her and caught her in his arms.

It was then, with the shock of his touch, that the force of attraction hit home. And the look of concern that appeared on his face transformed him from a tough and ornery cop into a sensitive guy, with the kind of animal magnetism that she rarely encountered. His dark blue eyes honed in on her and nearly took her breath away. Right there on the soccer field, in front of all those young, impressionable boys, including her own son, she found herself wondering what it would be like to have his lips connected to hers.

Instead, and in spite of the attraction, she hastily pulled away, somehow managing to mumble something about being able to take care of herself. Then, without looking at him or the boys, who no doubt were all eyes, she carefully marched off the field with all the dignity she could muster—no easy feat in those damnable three-inch heels.

Now here he was again, but at least on her turf. She rolled back her shoulders, cleared her throat, and prepared to deal with the man. He didn't need to know that the sight of him unraveled her carefully orchestrated composure and robbed her of her usual aplomb. She was working now and she needed every ounce of professionalism she could get if she was going to successfully represent David.

Chapter Two

The room was packed and the steady clamor of voices wouldn't cease until the judge appeared and the morning session began. Gerard Fitzpatrick slowly looked around, spotting a number of people he knew. Abruptly, he stopped halfway around the room and stared. There she was, Mary Ellen Carey. The one who had gotten him so stirred up the day before on the soccer field. Damn attractive, but out of his league and, from what he'd just learned, a major source of trouble.

He had just been informed by one of his men at the precinct that she had called there that morning—something to do with threatening phone calls and the Anderson kid. That could only mean problems, and was reason enough to resist her charms— of which she had many.

But that didn't keep him from appreciating the way her expensive clothes made a great body all the more intriguing. It didn't help that she was beautiful, in a classic, wholesome way, with porcelain skin and fine features. The fact that she didn't wear much makeup and still looked good would have driven his late wife nuts. But what drove him insane was her hair, a cloud of auburn curls that he wanted to crush in his hands, almost as much as he wanted to grab hold of that nicely toned body. It all spelled trouble.

But it wasn't just her looks. There was also something about her attitude: a lead from the chin, an I've-got-something-to-say-so-you-better-listen attitude, which really got under his skin. The fact that it came with an air of defenselessness was compelling and, though it was sexy in its way, was something he did not want to think about. She was not for him.

He hadn't always been so good at spotting her kind. But Donna, his late wife, had taught him well. The way this Mrs. (or was she a Ms.?) Carey looked in her traditional business suit and high heels was the look his wife, Donna, had always envied. That she never achieved it, according to Donna, was his fault. If he'd made a better buck, she used to say, she too could have afforded the spas and salons where all those privileged women went. He would have to steer clear of Mrs. Carey because of her client, but that didn't stop him from finding her intriguing.

None of that excused his performance the day before. He still couldn't figure out what had come over him and why he'd been so rude. He usually went out of his way to be polite to the parents, to establish trust. But for some reason, when she'd marched on the field, he'd lost all reason and behaved in a way that still made him cringe. He'd been hoping to forget it ever happened, but he knew he would have to say something to her, no matter what her involvement with Anderson. She was still one of his kids' mothers. Running into her in the courtroom was not what he'd had in mind. But he would bite the bullet and deal with her—before it got any worse.

"Mrs. Carey," he began, wishing himself a hundred miles away.

"Mary Ellen, please," she murmured, not looking particularly comfortable either. "Mrs. Carey is my ex-mother-in-law."

He nodded. "Of course," he mumbled. "And please, call me Fitz." He paused. "About yesterday. I'm sorry we got off on such a bad note."

Mary Ellen shook her head. It seemed like she was surprised and maybe even embarrassed that he'd brought it up. "I probably shouldn't have gone out on the field to speak to you in the middle of practice."

"No," he said, raising his hand in protest. "I was totally out of line. You had something to tell me."

She hadn't expected an apology judging from the way he'd behaved yesterday. But observing him now, standing before her, she started to wonder if perhaps he wasn't as cocky as she'd first imagined. What else would explain the way his hands kept moving through his thick, dark curls as he spoke? Based upon his previous behavior, she wouldn't have thought him the kind of man who would be nervous around a woman. Now that her eyes weren't clouded with irritation, she recognized that his rugged good looks were remarkable even in a courtroom filled with well-put-together lawyers. She'd have thought he was used to getting his way with women, and from the way he'd behaved yesterday, she also assumed he held them in low regard. Now she wasn't so sure. What she was sure of was that he was very attractive.

"So what brings you here?" he said.

"I have a pretrial hearing. What about you?"

"I'm scoping out some witnesses," he said, regarding her with such focus she wanted to run and hide. It had been a long time since a man had looked at her that way. Although she was flattered by his appreciative gaze, she wasn't used to it and suddenly felt self-conscious.

She wondered what his story was. She figured he was married, but a quick glance at his left hand told her that he didn't wear a wedding band. She didn't know much about him except that he was a cop and her son's soccer coach. He didn't look like a cop today, dressed in a well-tailored, navy blue suit, with a crisp white dress shirt that set off his tan. Even yesterday, in soccer shorts, solidly built and six feet something, he was a formidable presence. She was glad he couldn't read her mind. She wasn't interested in a relationship, but she would allow herself to fantasize.

"I take it Tim hasn't been on a soccer team before," he said.

She shook her head. "Until now he wasn't good enough to make the town's one team. We all appreciate your volunteering to coach," she added. It had been kind of him to step in. When the town recreation department saw how many boys wanted to play, they'd asked for a parent volunteer to coach a second team. Fitzpatrick was the only one who'd offered. Mary Ellen wanted him to know she was grateful.

"Tim's father and I divorced only last year, and now he's moved out of state," she said, wondering why she was explaining all this to a man she barely knew. "Tim hardly ever sees him. I appreciate any male influence." Somehow she didn't think living in an all-female household was the best situation for an eleven-year-old boy.

Fitz nodded. "I'm a single parent myself," he said. "My sons' mother passed away a few years ago," he added quickly. He seemed about to say something more, and in fact had leaned in her direction, as if what he had to say was for her ears only, when suddenly his eyes darkened and his expression changed from open, good-humored friendliness back to the wary look she remembered from the day before. Mary Ellen turned to see what might have caused the change, but there was only David Anderson heading toward them. She looked back at Fitz to continue their conversation, but he'd already stepped away, mumbling something about another courtroom.

It seemed like a peculiar reaction, and she wondered if he was always so erratic. But now was not the time to dwell on Coach Fitzpatrick. She needed to focus on David and his case. His name had just been called.

Chapter Three

This was not David's first visit to the courthouse. Mary Ellen had already represented him on a couple of incidents of underage drinking, one involving a party where the parents hadn't been home and the kids, including David, had trashed the house. Now that he was eighteen and old enough to be tried as an adult, the charges were more serious. As they walked up to the front of the courtroom, Mary Ellen noticed that David was trembling. She wasn't surprised. Although he often played the tough guy, she'd suspected otherwise.

They'd spent the previous afternoon going over the case, but seeing how nervous he was, Mary Ellen was afraid that David would stray from the truth if the judge asked him any questions.

She reached over and took his arm. "David," she whispered, "remember what I said about lying."

David looked over at her with wide, frightened eyes and nodded as Mary Ellen motioned for him to sit next to her at the defendant's table in the front of the courtroom. Harry Moore, one of the county prosecutors, was sitting at the opposite table. She recognized him from some cases they'd both been involved in. He was usually a reasonable man. David's biggest problem was Judge Dugan, who had a reputation for being tough.

The judge looked skeptical when Mary Ellen explained her position. He kept looking at David as if trying to assess the likelihood of David reforming if he didn't give him a tough sentence. Then he asked Mary Ellen if he could ask David a few questions.

She nodded and motioned for David to stand.

He stood up hesitantly and glanced over at Mary Ellen for reassurance. She did her best to look encouraging.

"Tell me exactly what happened," demanded the judge.

David managed to look nervous and defensive at the same time. "Didn't my lawyer?"

"Yes, but I'd like to hear your version, if you can manage it."

David nodded, looking as if maybe he couldn't.

"I was with my friends," he explained. "We'd all had too much to drink. You know how it can get."

Mary Ellen cringed, but the judge seemed to take David's comment in the intended manner and nodded as if he did indeed know how it could get.

David continued. "My pal Tony got into an argument with his girlfriend, Jess," he said, "and some other guy they knew. They started horsing around, but they were drunk, so it got a little rough. I grabbed Jess—to protect her, you know? Then other people got involved and the next thing I knew . . ."

The judge nodded and motioned for David to sit down. Mary Ellen wasn't sure if David had done himself any good and took her first opportunity to cut in and speak.

"My client does not deny anything, but he sincerely regrets the entire incident," she said.

"Then how would you suggest we proceed?" said the judge in a neutral tone, as if thinking about what David had told him.

"If it pleases the court and satisfies the prosecutor," she said, nodding in Moore's direction, "I would suggest that consideration be given to the fact that David has extensive ties in and about the area."

"So what are you asking? Dismiss the case because he's a hometown boy?" There was a definite edge to the judge's voice that made Mary Ellen uneasy.

"There is no dispute that he should pay for what he did," she said, "but since all of his friends and family are in West Orange, there is no reason to think he will leave the area. Besides, he just turned eighteen. Does he really deserve a criminal record for being stupid? Instead of jail time, it would be more appropriate for him to do community service, something that might teach him a lesson."

The judge raised his eyebrows and nodded. "Do you have any suggestions?" he asked, turning to Moore.

Moore shrugged. "We've got several playgrounds that could use work. The one over on Washington Street has park benches covered in graffiti. He could start by cleaning them. Sure," he said, after a slight hesitation, "community service sounds like a good idea."

Mary Ellen and Moore worked out that someone from the County Parks Department would contact her about the cleanup and the judge agreed to the plan.

Satisfied with the outcome, she quickly led David out of the courtroom. As an attorney, it was the best she could have expected. As a mother, she wouldn't have been happy if David had gotten off with only a slap on the wrist. He needed to grow up and learn that acts had consequences. David wasn't as pleased and was even whining about what they were going to make him do as they walked out.

When they got out into the hallway, David headed off to meet his parents, who were waiting outside. She was about to go back to the office when she bumped into John Susino, an old friend and classmate who now worked in the United States Attorney's office.

"When did you go back to criminal law?" he asked after greeting her.

"I didn't," she said. She was just about to tell him about David's case when Fitz came through the door.

There was no way he was going to be able to avoid her—not if she was with John. The woman was making him crazy. From the way they were standing there talking, it was obvious that she and John Susino, who was the most honorable of United States Attorneys, were good buddies. That did not jibe with her representation of the Anderson kid. But ever since talking to her, he hadn't been able to figure out her connection with Anderson. At the very least, the boy was mixed up with a tough crowd. So why was this classy woman representing the kid in court?

But there was no way he could avoid John, and maybe if he spent a little time with this Carey woman, he would be able to figure her out.

He went over and lightly tapped John on the shoulder. John greeted him with an easy smile and then turned to Mary Ellen. "Have you met the boys' soccer coach?"

Maybe that was his connection with Carey. Both Susino's son and hers were on the team. The boys probably were friends.

Mary Ellen nodded. "Yesterday at practice," she and Fitz said simultaneously.

Susino turned and waved to someone on the other side of the hall. "I've been trying to reach that guy for weeks. Excuse me for a second? I just want to run over and grab him while I can. Then let's get lunch? My treat."

After John left, Mary Ellen stood and stared at Fitz. He had thus far been so unpredictable, she didn't know what to say for fear of his reaction.

He scowled. "You might want to be a bit more careful about who you represent." He spoke almost in a whisper, his eyes on the floor. She could barely make out his words, but he was clearly agitated.

"I beg your pardon? Who are you to tell me who I can and cannot represent?" They were strong words that betrayed her lingering uneasiness from the phone call that morning. Maybe it wasn't a joke. The call had to be about David. But that still didn't make sense, unless it was one of his friends' misguided efforts to help. "Exactly what do you mean?"

Fitz shrugged, seemingly unperturbed by her response. "Weren't you just with the Anderson kid? From what I hear about him and his buddies, they are not the kind of client someone like you would want to be connected with."

"Is that right?" she said. "How would you know what kind of client I would want?"

"I got the impression that you do mostly corporate law. I'm wondering if a kid like David Anderson is what you're used to. I'm just suggesting that you might be in over your head. I'm not trying to interfere or tell you how to run your business, but he does have some tough connections." He looked around uneasily, as if searching for an escape. "Would you tell John I had to run? There are places I need to be."

She nodded. She was irritated but felt uneasy as well. When John returned, she didn't say anything about their conversation except to explain that Fitz couldn't do lunch. But she couldn't help worrying. Was there more going on with David than she knew? First the call this morning, and now Fitz's warning. But David Anderson was inept. How could he be involved in anything serious?

John Susino, meanwhile, was shepherding her out the door and down the stairs to the street. "Before we run into anyone else," he explained.

She gratefully agreed. A quiet lunch was what she needed,

that and the reassurance that her kids were okay. She called Heidi from the restaurant and determined that the children were fine. When she sat down at the table with John, his first question was about Fitz.

"What's with you two?" he asked.

She shook her head. "You noticed? I don't know what his beef is."

"I can't understand it," said John, shaking his head. "Besides being a great coach, Fitz has to be one of the nicest guys I know. I would have thought the two of you would have a lot in common." These last words were accompanied by a meaningful look.

A waiter came over to their table, so they both quickly scanned their menus and gave their orders. When he departed, Mary Ellen turned to John, wagging her index finger at him. "Don't get any ideas about fixing me up. I have enough problems in my life without adding men to the equation."

John shook his head. "It's been a year," he said. "Aren't you ever going to come out of hiding? You're only thirty-eight. It seems a little early to pack it in."

"Well, forget Fitz," said Mary Ellen. She made a face. "Besides, after what's gone on between us, I think it's rather unlikely."

"What happened, anyway?" asked John.

Mary Ellen explained about their meeting on the soccer field. "Tim didn't want me to go out there, but I was afraid he'd be too bashful to tell Fitz himself." She realized that she probably should have trusted Tim more. He was eleven. But it was so hard to let kids grow up, particularly when they were all you had.

John just grinned. "Maybe he does come on a bit strong sometimes. He has very definite ideas about coaching. But he really is a good guy."

"I'm glad to hear it," she said. "But I'm not sure what, if anything, that has to do with me."

He shrugged. "You want me to butt out, is that it?" He was silent for a minute before continuing. "Maybe I should. But I worry about you. I can't believe you don't want something more." He took a sip of his water. "Maybe it's just that I hate to see you alone."

Mary Ellen didn't know how to respond, so it was fortunate that their food arrived just then, providing her with an excuse not to answer.

"You can't go blaming every guy you run into for what your ex did," John said between mouthfuls, not ready to give up. "You're still young and attractive. Don't throw it away because of a jerk like that. Besides, you've got your kids to think about."

"My kids? What do they have to do with my dating?"

"Wouldn't they be better off if you were happy? Had a full life?"

She stared at him, not answering. What gave him the right to tell her what she needed? Nothing, but maybe there was something to what he said. It wasn't such a great lesson to her kids to see her grow angry and bitter. Maybe she should reconsider her decision to eliminate men from her life. But she wasn't sure if she was ready just yet.

Chapter Four

When Mary Ellen walked back into the office, her secretary was anxiously waiting. "Mr. Dunphy wants to see you immediately. He says it's urgent."

She rushed down the hall to find him. As the senior partner of the firm, Dunphy rarely involved himself in day-to-day activities. Sometimes she didn't see him for weeks at a time. It had to be serious.

She found him pacing back and forth in front of his office, chewing nervously on his unlit pipe. He wore a pink polo shirt that picked up a dominant color in the madras plaid of his slacks. Mary Ellen assumed he had a golf date later that afternoon. He usually did.

"Thank God you're back!" he exclaimed, raising his hands dramatically. "Get in here." He pointed to his office. "We've got a real problem."

"What's going on?" she asked.

It was something serious—that was clear. He motioned for her to sit down in the chair across from his desk and closed the door behind him.

"When the Andersons got back from lunch today with David," Dunphy began, "they were greeted by a U.S. Marshal and two officers who took David into custody."

"David's been arrested? We were just in court this morning. We took care of the charge against him."

Dunphy shook his head. "It's a different case. This was a warrant from the United States Attorney's office. Kirk Anderson was so upset when he called that he barely made sense, but it sounds like they're accusing David of racketeering."

This must be what the call had been about. It was much more serious than wrecking a bar. She remembered Fitz's warnings about the guys David was mixed up with. Her children could be in real trouble.

"Mary Ellen? Are you even listening to me?" Dunphy asked. "This is serious! You've got to go down there and get David released immediately!"

She wasn't listening. She was thinking about her children. She had to make sure they were safe. She didn't have time to go down to the courthouse and bail out David.

But she must appear calm. She didn't want to give Dunphy an excuse to favor one of the male associates. She remembered that one of them, Michael Stein, was in court this afternoon. She knew because she'd run into him on his way there. She told Dunphy, "Why don't we get Stein to bail David out?"

Dunphy looked skeptical.

"If Michael is already down there, it would be faster. If David has to wait for me, he might be there all afternoon."

Dunphy nodded. "Maybe you're right. Can we get hold of Michael?"

"Sure. I'll just get his cell phone number from his secretary. If he doesn't answer, there's always the court clerk. We'll find him."

"Okay. Sounds reasonable. I'll call Kirk Anderson and tell him what we're doing." He picked up the phone, punched in a few numbers, and after a pause, frowned. "Phone's busy. I'll try again in a few minutes."

"Why don't I call him? Just tell me what he's told you. Did he give you any specifics about the charges against David?"

"Not much. He was upset. He did say something about David being called the mastermind behind a car theft ring in Essex County."

"Mastermind? David? It's hard to imagine David organizing an excursion to the men's room, much less something as complicated as that."

He shrugged.

"He's certainly no Rhodes Scholar. But they must have something on him, or he wouldn't have been indicted," she said. "Don't you think the Andersons should have a high-powered criminal attorney? This could be serious."

Dunphy shook his head. "Anderson won't hear of it. Said you'd always done just fine. Insists he has total confidence in you now and is optimistic that the case will be dismissed."

Mary Ellen cringed. She was afraid he'd have that reaction. Since the first time she'd represented David, his father had insisted she handle all his matters.

"I'll call him now and have him fax me a copy of the indictment," she said. "But I'm afraid this isn't going to be an easy fix. There's got to be something to this or they wouldn't have been able to get a warrant."

"That's not what Anderson thinks. He was sputtering about David being set up. That this court business is a plot to intimidate Anderson to keep him from putting up the new building he's got planned for Florham Park. The bad publicity could make it impossible for him to get the variances he needs and, of course, the financing."

"You mean because the town officials and local banks would be afraid to be involved with him on account of his son?"

"Exactly," said Dunphy with a nod.

She shook her head. "That's hardly likely," she said. "What did you tell him?"

"That I would talk to you."

"Great! You want me to talk to him."

"You know more about the criminal justice system."

"Mr. Dunphy—"

"I know you can handle this." He met her eyes, his expression serious. "I don't have to tell you that Anderson is our biggest client, and if you do well, you'll be our golden girl, but if you bungle it—" He paused and shook his head before continuing. "I don't know what will happen."

She suppressed a sigh. Anderson's company supplied more than half the work in the firm.

Dunphy continued. "There's got to be a way to get David out of this thing. You've got contacts. Just start thinking about who you know and what strings you might pull. For starters, there's your buddy in the U.S. Attorney's office."

She nodded. She knew he meant John Susino.

"Talk to him," said Dunphy. "Maybe he'll tell you what's going on." He stood up. "You've got a few calls to make and I have a tee time at three." He paused as he looked at his watch, signaling her dismissal. "I've got to run. I have every confidence that you can handle this to Anderson's satisfaction."

Mary Ellen nodded, wishing it were that simple.

Back in her office, she began to make her calls. She had to get in touch with Michael Stein and Kirk Anderson before she could leave and find her children.

The first call was easy. Michael answered his phone on the initial ring. When she told him what was going on, he agreed to cover the arraignment and bail hearing and get David released.

The next call was more difficult. "I'm totally convinced of his innocence," said Mr. Anderson. "The kid's been set up. Mary

Ellen—" He paused to catch his breath, clearly agitated. "You know how gullible he is, gullible and weak. But he's not a thief."

"I don't think so either. But that's what he's been charged with, so we need to deal with it. I've got to talk to him. Get his version. Hopefully he'll be able to explain what is really going on so I can prepare a defense."

"You're to get him off. I don't care how you do it or what it costs. There's got to be some way. Dunphy said you knew some people down in the U.S. Attorney's office. Anything I can do to convince them to help us?"

Mary Ellen tried to ignore the implication. "I do have a friend there, but it would be inappropriate for you to speak to him about the case," said Mary Ellen. "And that's not going to solve our problem anyway. What I need to do is talk to David."

"Maybe," he said reluctantly. "But first we need to get him home. I'm sure after what he's been through, he'll be rattled. Why don't I bring him over to your office tomorrow?"

"That would be fine," she said. "I can call him first thing in the morning and arrange it. It would be better to see him alone," she added carefully. She would get more from David if he was not with his father, but she couldn't offend Anderson. "Now that he's eighteen and is treated as an adult in the court system, maybe we should encourage him to act like one."

"Maybe," he repeated, sounding doubtful.

As soon as the call ended, she stood up. Now she needed to get out of there. She called Heidi from her cell phone as she made her way to the parking deck to make sure they were all waiting for her at the pool. There was no answer. Frantically, she redialed. After several tries, she still couldn't get through. There had to be a reasonable explanation, but thoughts of the morning's call and the reality of the trouble David was in kept intruding. Heidi was usually very responsible. It wasn't like her to ignore the phone. Something had to be wrong. After the fourth try, she phoned the Maplewood police station and reported the threatening call to the desk sergeant.

"My children are supposed to be at the town pool with their sitter, but they're not answering," she said, explaining about the cell phone that Heidi promised to keep by her side throughout the day.

The sergeant sounded sympathetic. He must have kids of his own. "I was going to swing by anyway," he said. "I'll meet you over there."

Her head pounding, almost too frantic to think, Mary Ellen raced to her car and in minutes was on Route 78 trying not to wonder if she was already too late. She was forced to slow down when she hit the local streets of Maplewood and was panicking by the time she turned into the municipal lot and observed several squad cars parked right by the pool's entrance. Afraid to waste a minute, she pulled up right alongside. She put the car in park, not bothering to turn off the engine, and bolted through the gates to the pool area.

Once inside, she frantically looked around for something resembling a hostage situation. Other than the cop cars outside, though, the scene looked deceptively normal. Until she looked over at the snack bar, where she saw four uniformed officers and Fitz, still in his blue suit, surrounding Heidi and her three children, who all looked bewildered.

Chapter Five

Fitz had been on his way home early. Because it was a hot Friday in the summer, he figured he'd meet his boys at the pool, have a swim, and then take them out for pizza. He had his police radio on in the car out of habit.

"This is car eighty-eight. Heading over to the municipal pool in response to an urgent phone call from resident Mary Ellen Carey, who believes her children may be in trouble. Don't know how serious a threat it is, but I'm checking it out."

He recognized the voice as belonging to Sergeant Joe Maloney. Without having to think about it, he found himself speeding through the streets of Maplewood toward the pool.

Even as he pulled up to the front entrance, it was clear there was no crisis. And when he parked and entered the main pool area, there was nothing out of the ordinary. He saw Maloney talking to a crowd of children, including Tim, and headed in that direction. By the time he got over there, the children had all dispersed except for Tim, two teenage girls who he assumed were Tim's sisters, and an older girl who was probably the kids' sitter.

Maloney and Fitz greeted each other and Fitz asked him

what happened, briefly explaining that he knew the children's mother through work and Tim through soccer.

Maloney shrugged and shook his head, looking almost amused. "I got the call at the station house," he said. "She sounded frantic, but not unbalanced, if you know what I mean." Fitz nodded.

Maloney continued, explaining that the sitter had been swimming when Mary Ellen called and no one had heard the phone ring. "That isn't unusual," concluded Maloney. "We get plenty of calls from overanxious parents. It's just that she didn't seem to fit that profile. I wouldn't have rushed over here if she had."

Fitz agreed. It was exactly what he had been thinking. Why had Ms. Carey pushed the panic button? She didn't seem like the hysterical sort. From what he knew of her, she was far from it. Since their meeting earlier in the day, he had made a few discreet inquiries and had learned that Mary Ellen Carey was more experienced in criminal law than he'd first thought. She had been an Assistant District Attorney in Brooklyn. She would know if there was a reason to be worried. So what made her panic and call the police? There it was again. Something was going on with the Anderson case.

When she arrived at the pool, he spotted her immediately. Even from a distance, her concern was clear from the way she dashed in, her eyes moving over the crowd as if she was searching for someone or something. She eased up some when she spotted her children, although he knew from her furrowed eyebrows and pursed lips that she was still worried.

He couldn't take his eyes off her. He knew he should be suspicious. He didn't trust her client. But his gut told him she was okay, that she wasn't who he'd first imagined her to be. He watched her stride over to where they were standing and sweep three nearly full-grown adolescents into her arms, ignoring their soaking-wet bodies.

He wished he were part of that scene, that his kids had that kind of mother. When he pictured her reading to them at night, just before she shut off their lights, he forced himself to change gears. This wasn't personal, he sharply reminded himself. She was involved with one of his chief suspects. What he needed to focus on was what frightened her enough to call the police.

Mary Ellen realized she needed to get a grip when she saw her children's reactions. They were good sports about the hugs, even Tim, but mortified about her alerting the police.

"Mother! What were you thinking?" said Anna. "Have you finally lost your mind? Should we start calling you every time we make a move?"

The other two nodded. For once all three seemed to be in agreement.

"I was concerned," she started to explain, until she realized that unless they knew about the threatening call, they wouldn't understand. "I guess I may have overreacted," she conceded. "When I couldn't get ahold of Heidi, I suddenly had visions of something awful happening to you. But of course, that's ridiculous and probably has more to do with all I have on my mind to prepare for our vacation."

The three looked somewhat mollified, Tim particularly. He was always the quickest to forgive. She knew the other two would hold out a little longer. "You staying for the meet?" he asked, suddenly looking up at the clock on the front of the building.

She nodded, relieved to change the subject. "Of course. If you are supposed to be with your team, go on over. I'll be fine. I'd better park the car. Then I'll probably go for a quick swim before I settle in to watch." She wished there was a way to erase what had happened, starting with that phone call. She didn't want them worried—about her or what might be happening. "Shall we go for pizza afterward?" she asked, calling after them. When the three nodded enthusiastically, she once again thanked God for what seemed to be the perfect teenage food.

After she parked, she went to the ladies' locker room and changed into the bathing suit that she always kept in the car. One positive lesson from all she had gone through with her husband was that a few laps, on a regular basis, did wonders for relieving stress. She figured there was just enough time to swim before the kids' meet started.

Unfortunately, even after several laps, her mind was still working even overtime. It was going to take more than exercise to get her back to normal after the day she'd had. But she needed to get a grip before she did something crazy. The last thing she wanted to do was frighten her children. She was determined not to act like someone whose offspring had been threatened.

It was in the middle of all this self-analysis that she felt a sharp tug. At first she ignored it, and when the tug persisted, she took her head out of the water and turned around in annoyance. But when she saw that it was Fitz, treading water beside her, a concerned look on his face, her irritation dissipated and the underlying fear resurfaced. Now what?

"We've got to talk!" he said, his voice tense but determined.

Automatically she shook her head.

He reached over and took her hand so she couldn't swim away. "It's important. You may be in more danger than you think."

She looked down at his hand on hers and then back up at him. Why this sudden concern? He was practically a stranger. She was about to tell him to let go, but stopped. She wasn't so sure she wanted him to leave. When she looked into his eyes, she saw only sincerity. Besides, he seemed to know more about David and the crowd he hung out with than anyone else. That he looked very good standing there in the shallow end of the pool, where she'd reluctantly followed him, with water running down his solid, muscular chest, was something she couldn't allow herself to dwell on. He was just an ordinary guy, she reminded herself, and patronizing at that. But as she looked up into his dark blue eyes, she wasn't totally convinced.

"Is this about David Anderson?" she said.

He nodded.

"What's going on? What do you know about David that I don't?"

"You shouldn't be involved with him," he said, ignoring her question. "You're in way over your head."

"You don't know anything about me," she said, irritated that he assumed she couldn't handle David's case. Maybe she was a bit out of practice, but when she was an Assistant District Attorney in Brooklyn, she'd successfully handled plenty of serious cases.

"I'm not trying to insult you," he said. "You just don't know who you're dealing with and to what lengths these guys will go."

"What do you mean 'guys'?" she asked. "You still haven't told me who these people are. Why should I be worried?"

He didn't immediately answer, but instead stared with eyes warm with what might have been compassion. "I can't say," he said. "But you need to know this case is much bigger than you think and it involves a lot more than just an eighteen-year-old punk and his buddies. As I said, you shouldn't be involved."

She shook her head. "I can't get out of it," she said. "Even if you're right, I can't just disengage myself. He's my client. I represent him."

She paused as she wondered how much to tell him. Her children could really be in danger, he was a cop, and she couldn't protect them alone. "Assuming you're correct," she said slowly, her voice barely above a whisper, "what do I do? I mean, if you were me and you got a call about your children—"

His hand, which was still on hers, tightened its grip and his eyes narrowed. "They threatened your children?"

She hesitated before nodding.

He shook his head. "You have to get off the case."

It was her turn to shake her head. "You're not listening to me! I just finished telling you, I can't. I would need the court's permission, and the judge would never allow me to unless the client agreed. He won't."

"Then you have to get your children out of here. Send them away."

She nodded. She knew he was right. That was exactly what she had to do. But not yet. Not until after the vacation. She explained to Fitz that they were going away, just a week. "We rented a house on Long Beach Island," she said. "We've looked forward to it all year." She realized how lame that sounded. Her children could be in real danger and here she was talking about a vacation!

"Does anyone know you're going?" he asked.

She nodded. "Half the town, probably. The whole office, anyway, and our friends. You know what it's like around here."

He was quiet for a minute, thinking. "What if you went somewhere else?"

"What do you mean?"

"What if you still went away, just not to Long Beach Island? But you didn't tell anyone, not even your children?"

"How am I going to do that?"

"I know a place," he said, "down in North Carolina. You could go there."

"I can't do that."

"Why not?"

"I hardly know you!"

"Even if it means protecting your children? I'm a cop. You can trust me."

She didn't answer, thinking about what he said. He was probably right. If there was anyone she should be able to trust . . . "I just can't do it," she said automatically, the words forming without her having to think about them. She had always been independent—even more so since the divorce. It was a basic part of her personality. "Thanks for the offer," she added quickly. "I do appreciate it, but I'll have to solve this one myself. Somehow."

"You don't have to be in this by yourself. I can help you."

She frowned and shook her head.

"Is it because you don't trust me?"

She looked at him in surprise. She realized that wasn't the case. He was practically a stranger and she didn't have any reason to trust him, but the truth of the matter was that she did trust him. When she looked into his eyes, she saw something that made her believe not only that he was above reproach, but that he could and would help her—if she let him.

But she still couldn't accept his offer.

"There's no way I can convince you?"

She shook her head. She had to get away from him before she gave in to the temptation and let him. "I'd better get over to this swim meet. It looks like it's about to start."

He nodded and let go of her hand. He was about to dive in and swim away when she stopped him, reaching out and touching his arm. "I do appreciate the offer. It was very kind of you. And believe me, I am taking this threat seriously. I just haven't had time to figure out what to do. But I will." She paused before continuing. "I've been on my own long enough to learn how to take care of myself and my babies."

Chapter Six

Mary Ellen," said her secretary, Marge, "there's someone on line two. Says he's calling about the Anderson case. Should I put him through?"

"Go ahead." She had the file before her now, reviewing the court papers while she waited for David. She expected him shortly. Maybe it was someone from the U.S. Attorney's office wanting to discuss the case, or even to make a deal, though at this early stage that was unlikely.

She recognized that voice instantly, low and slow, again sounding like a bad connection. "Just a reminder," the caller said with deceptive calmness. "Get David off, or your kids are in danger."

"Who is this?"

"You don't need to know that," he said. "What you gotta know is that we're serious when we say we'll hurt your children. Get the Anderson kid off. Got that?"

His last words were followed by a dial tone. She sat listening to it, frozen to the chair. What was she going to do? What kind of people had David gotten himself mixed up with? Fitz knew. She had to talk to him. Frantically, she pulled out her organizer and searched for the soccer roster with Fitz's work phone number. With shaking hands, she dialed his number. He had offered and she needed his help, she reminded herself, as she waited for him to answer.

After three rings, the call went to voice mail. Reluctantly, she left a message for him to call her.

What next? There had to be something she could do, someone to tell. This was suburban New Jersey. She was a lawyer. People like her didn't get threats about their children!

Mr. Dunphy! She'd speak to Mr. Dunphy. He was an old friend of Kirk Anderson and a powerful member of the New Jersey Bar Association. He might not like it, but she was sure that once she explained what was happening he would take her off the case. He could give it to someone who didn't have kids. She threw David's file, which she still had in her hand, on her cluttered desk and went to find him.

"Rosemary?" she said, looking questioningly at Dunphy's secretary after finding his office empty and his lights off. "Is Mr. Dunphy not in today?"

Rosemary shook her head. "Europe. He took Mrs. D. to Ireland."

Her heart sank. "Is he going to call in?" she asked, already knowing the answer.

"Not if Mrs. D. has anything to say about it," said Rosemary, smiling.

Frustrated, Mary Ellen went back to her office, sat down at her desk, and numbly opened David's file, pulling out her copy of the indictment. She'd read through the charges while she waited for David and tried not to think about the threatening calls. They had to do with David, she reminded herself. He must know what was going on. She would get to the bottom of this when he came in to see her.

The gist of the allegation against David was that he was the head of a car theft ring in northern New Jersey. It was also alleged that the stolen vehicles were taken to a chop shop and dismantled. The parts were then taken to Port Elizabeth and loaded into containers that were stowed aboard ships bound for Europe and South America. The location of the chop shop was listed, a side street off Bloomfield Avenue, in Bloomfield, New Jersey, along with the names and addresses of several container and shipping companies. She wondered how her caller fit in to this operation and whose orders he was following.

Whoever the caller was, he had a reason to be nervous about this case because it looked, at least from the detailed complaint, as if the government had solid evidence. If they'd put this much detail into the complaint, they probably had more. Reading between the lines, it was obvious that they had at least one source. Could that be someone connected to David?

What puzzled her right now was how David had gotten himself involved in such a sophisticated operation. David didn't have much in the way of brains and was not a leader. From what she could see, he was usually the one left holding the bag. It had happened most recently when he had gone with his friends to that bar and had gotten into a brawl. David was the only one arrested, but he obviously hadn't been there alone. Perhaps that had happened this time as well.

She looked at her watch. David was fifteen minutes late. She drummed her fingers in agitation. She needed to talk to him to see if he could identify her caller. Even if he couldn't, if she could resolve David's situation, maybe the threat to her children would go away.

The phone rang. It was Kirk Anderson.

"What can I do for you?" she asked, hoping she didn't sound as stressed as she felt.

"I want to talk about this case against David," he shouted in his usual blustering manner.

"I'm expecting him any moment. Why don't I talk to you after I see him?"

"He won't be coming."

"What? We had an appointment."

"I know," said Anderson with exaggerated patience. "That's why I'm calling. David won't be there. I decided it would be better if you and I talk first. The boy doesn't always know what's good for him."

"I don't understand. I'm his attorney. If either of you is not happy with my representation, you should get someone else. This case is too big for you not to be completely satisfied with your representation."

"I want you as our attorney. You've always done a good job. There's no reason to switch."

She swallowed her protest. "Thank you for your confidence. But if you want me to represent him, I must speak with him."

"Not until I've spoken to you first. After that, he's yours."

What he said made her uneasy. Was it possible that he had some connection with the phone calls? Possible, but improbable. Kirk Anderson was an old friend of Mr. Dunphy's and a respected member of the community, not some lowlife who went around threatening other people's children.

"First we need to have a simple understanding," said Anderson. "He's innocent, and I want him off. I don't need to know the details or how or what you do to make that happen. Are we clear on that? I just want his name cleared. And I don't want him to testify."

"He doesn't have to testify. He can plead the Fifth. But since he's named as a defendant and has been properly served, he's got to respond in some way, or else he'll be in contempt. Whether he did it or not, he still has to appear in court. If he doesn't, he'll be in even more trouble."

"All right, I hear you. So when's the hearing?"

"A week from this Tuesday."

"He can be there. But you don't need to talk to him before that."

"I have to talk to him," she insisted as Anderson talked over her protests with a long explanation as to why it would be better if David didn't meet with her. She realized that arguing with Anderson was futile. She would just have to try to call David directly.

"You can meet him in the courthouse. And the wife and I will be there. This is too important for you to exclude us."

"I'm not trying to exclude you," she protested. "I'd just need to speak with him in private before the hearing."

"And I'm telling you we'll get there in enough time for you to prepare him. I know you don't want David to say something stupid, but I don't want him getting all confused. If you prepare him just before he sees the judge, he should be okay. You know how he is. The courthouse intimidates him. He gets scared and flustered and says the wrong thing. If he's got to be there, then he should be with his parents. Besides, he's innocent. I've talked to him, and he says he doesn't know anything about this car thing."

She started to respond, but again Anderson interrupted. "David's word is good enough for me, and it should be good enough for you."

She didn't argue. She would just have to figure a way around him so she could get David alone before they went before the judge. Otherwise, who knew what he would say.

Mary Ellen hung up realizing that she still didn't know who was behind the threatening calls and she wasn't going to find out.

Chapter Seven

Fitz had called while she was on the phone with Anderson. She called him back. When he answered, she quickly explained about the second threatening call.

"Meet me after work," he said. "At the new coffeehouse in town across from the train station. You know where I mean, right? Six o'clock."

This was a man used to giving orders. She wondered why she wasn't annoyed.

Fitz got there first and chose a table in the far corner of the restaurant. Automatically he sat down with his back to the wall. He spotted Mary Ellen when she first walked in, before she saw him. He liked having a chance to appreciate the way the short yellow dress showed off her legs and clung to her trim figure. He forced himself not to stare as she walked to the table, even as he noted that the V-neckline of her dress revealed a little cleavage. This woman, he reminded himself, was here because she needed his help.

* * *

When she saw Fitz in the restaurant, Mary Ellen was almost amused. Leave it to a cop to sit with his back to the wall, all the better to spot any trouble. But at least he wasn't sitting by the window. In a small town like theirs, there would be talk if anyone saw them together.

She was also happy that she'd taken the time to change out of her serious navy courtroom suit and had put on something cool and easy. Fitz was wearing shorts and a gray T-shirt, and she couldn't help but notice that he looked very good, especially when he stood to greet her and she had a look at the whole of him.

"Wait until they take our order before you tell me about the calls," he said, looking around the restaurant for a server. "Try to remember everything. You never know what might be important," he added as he signaled for service. "Coffee?" he asked Mary Ellen as the teenage server approached.

She nodded. "A large iced latte. Please."

He ordered a regular iced coffee for himself. "Anything to eat?"

She shook her head. "I couldn't."

He nodded. "Too upset to eat?"

She nodded.

"Try and calm down so we can plan this. But first, tell me what the caller said."

She recounted the call, doing her best to remember the man's exact words.

"Same guy, huh? What'd he sound like? Young, old, accent, anything unusual?"

She closed her eyes and forced herself to remember. "I think he was definitely older than David and his friends, and from his accent, he's from around here," she said. "That's all," she added, frustrated because she couldn't be more helpful.

He reached over, took her hand, and squeezed it reassuringly. "We'll figure this out. They won't get your children. I promise."

She nodded, finding comfort in his touch. Nice, almost too nice if she was going to have to stay alert and focus on the problem in front of her.

"Do you have any idea who it could be?" she asked as she gently removed her hand from his. "Do you think he's one of the people involved with David?" She paused and took a deep breath.

Fitz shrugged. "I don't know who the caller is, but I have my suspicions. But I think, for the time being," he said hesitantly, as if thinking it through as he spoke, "it's best if I don't tell you anything except what you need to know to keep your children safe. Besides, as I said before, I'm not really at liberty to discuss the case from our end, and you are still his attorney." He smiled, as if to reassure her that this didn't mean they were adversaries. "Anyway, it'll make it easier when you talk to your children."

She guessed what he'd said made sense. "But my children. How am I going to protect them? Do you have a plan?"

He nodded. "The offer stands for you to take that place on the Outer Banks in North Carolina." He looked up and met her eyes. "It's really not so different from the Jersey shore, just further away."

"So what are you suggesting? That I drive down there tonight, instead of going to Long Beach Island?"

"Yeah. Do you think you could do that?"

"I guess," she said, thinking about the additional ten hours of driving that would require. "Even if we left here at seven tonight, like we planned, we wouldn't get there until three or four in the morning, depending on traffic."

He nodded. "Too much driving. You should probably stay in a hotel along the way. Maybe in Maryland. Here, I brought a map to show you the route."

He pulled a small road atlas out of his pocket, moved his chair closer to hers, and put the map between them, at the edge of the table, as if afraid someone would see what they were looking at. The thought sent a chill right through her. What were they up against?

She had to lean toward him to see the map. She caught his scent and felt his bare leg as it brushed hers. Her pulse beat faster, her breathing quickened. Even as tense as she was, it was impossible to deny the chemistry between them. Which may have been why she was unnerved when he said he'd also be coming down to the beach house.

"You're staying there too?" she said, hoping her face didn't reflect her thoughts.

He nodded. "Yeah, with my boys. I've got two," he added when she shot him a questioning look. "Robby, who's on the soccer team with Tim, and Mike. He's eight."

So his wife had left him with two young sons. That was tough. She wondered how he'd coped and if his boys had recovered from the loss. Losing your mother like that had to be horrible. Worse than having your dad walk out. And she thought her kids had it rough.

Their coffees arrived, which gave her a chance to collect her thoughts and think about his suggestion to stay with him. She hardly knew him, never mind that she found him attractive.

"I know this is awkward," he said, perhaps sensing her hesitation. "But your children will be even safer with me there than you would be by yourselves."

She nodded. There was no denying that it made sense. And the drive wasn't all that bad, especially if she stopped and broke up the trip.

She took a sip of her latte and then looked up at him. "I'll do it," she said. "I think you're right. I don't see any other way." Not with someone out there threatening her children.

He smiled, obviously relieved. "That's how I see it." He reached into his pocket and pulled out a wad of papers. "I've got directions here someplace, from the Interstate, and the address of the house." He found the piece of paper and handed it to her.

She read through the directions while he explained. "The house is on the main drag, so you won't have any trouble finding it. It's a nice place," he added, looking at her as if trying to reassure her. "It's right on the ocean, and there are four good-sized bedrooms and a couple of bathrooms, so there will be plenty of room for everyone."

"Sounds fine," she said, unable to concentrate on the layout of the house or the directions in front of her. She was struggling with the fact that she'd just agreed to spend the week sharing a house with this very attractive man. And with her leg touching his, she knew that the physical attraction was not something she could easily ignore.

But she would certainly try. "Who owns the house?" she asked. Maybe it belonged to his girlfriend, and she could stop her fantasies.

"Terry Jones, a friend of mine from high school who moved down that way."

Terry? Aha, she was right, there was someone, and here she had been doing all this worrying for nothing. She looked up at him. "Will she be there too?"

He looked puzzled for an instant. "She?" Then he suddenly smiled, as if understanding. "Terry's a guy. Stands for Terrance, and to answer your question, no, he won't be there. He uses the place in June and September and rents it out the rest of the time. I did him a favor once and this is how he pays me back." He continued to look amused, much to her chagrin, but she did her best to ignore his reaction.

"I plan on leaving first thing tomorrow morning," he continued. "Since you'll get there before us, take this key," he added, reaching under the table and slipping it into her hand and closing her fingers around it.

Again she felt a current of electricity pass between them. She needed to learn how to ignore that attraction if she was going to be spending so much time with him. She looked over to see if he felt it too. Was she imagining the slight flush that had suddenly appeared on his face?

"There's a Holiday Inn in Maryland," he said, "about an hour after you get off the Cape May ferry, if you go that way. You'll also pass it if you take I-Ninety-Five. Why don't I make a reservation for you? That way you won't have to let your children know what's going on until you're well on your way."

That made sense. They'd be able to get going much faster if they didn't know there was a change in plans.

"Just as a precaution," he added, seeming to hesitate, "don't make the reservation in your name."

She looked at him, startled.

He pressed his lips together and didn't say anything for a minute. "I'm sure there's nothing to worry about, but why take chances?"

She smiled weakly, trying to force herself to believe that's all it was.

"O'Mara," he said, suddenly smiling. "I'll make it under my grandmother's name, Katie O'Mara. Okay?" He reached over and touched a strand of her hair. "With your red hair," he added, "they'll believe it. Don't you think?"

She nodded. She must have looked as frightened as she felt. But his efforts to soothe her didn't really help, particularly not after his next suggestion.

"We have to talk about how you are going to get down there."

"What do you mean?" Hadn't they just agreed that she would drive?

"Just in case you're being watched," he said with some hesitation, "I think you should take someone else's car."

She shook her head. She couldn't believe he thought things were that serious.

"I would rather err on the side of caution than be sorry afterward," he said, as if sensing her concerns.

She nodded, wondering if he was being too cautious. Besides, whose car could she borrow? Most people would hesitate to lend a car to someone going out of state for a week.

"What about your sitter's car? Couldn't you trade cars with her? It's really not for so long," he said, as if reading her thoughts.

"I guess." She thought about Heidi's loaded Grand Am and smiled. It would be tight in the two-door vehicle and they'd have to pack light, but her kids would appreciate the sound system. The only real issue was how Heidi would feel about driving a five-year-old Volvo. There was only one way to find out. At his suggestion, she excused herself, went outside and, after making sure no one was in hearing distance, called Heidi.

Even with little explanation, Heidi was perfectly amenable to the idea. Mary Ellen gratefully vowed to make it up to her when all of this was over.

When she got back to the table, they finished making plans. Fitz suggested she leave town in her own car and make the exchange later, halfway down the parkway at a rest stop. She didn't understand the secrecy and subterfuge, but Fitz was deadly serious.

"Coffee's on me," he said as they stood up to leave. She was just reaching for her purse.

She forced herself to smile. "I seem to have a lot to thank you for. How can I ever repay you?" she whispered.

He reached over and squeezed her hand. "Just be careful," he said, so softly she had to lean in to hear him. "Keep alert. I'm not sure how closely they're watching you."

She looked at him sharply. What kind of danger was she exposing her family to?

Chapter Eight

Two hours later, Mary Ellen pulled out of her driveway. As she buckled her seat belt, she reviewed her list of to-dos. The car was packed with their luggage, reduced by half so that it could all fit into Heidi's car. She had arranged for Mr. Taylor, their neighbor across the street, to take care of the cats. The paper was canceled; the mail held. The alarm was set and she had even watered all the plants. Their lives might be in jeopardy, but she was keeping everything in order.

She hadn't told the children what was going on. She wouldn't, even after they were on the parkway, bound for the rest stop where they would do the car exchange with Heidi. All three had fallen asleep as soon as they were on the road, and she had a brief reprieve.

While the children napped, she thought about what to tell them. Just enough, she figured, for them to realize they had to be careful, but not enough to unduly frighten them.

As she pulled into the stop, they began to wake up.

"Are we almost there?" Tim asked, his voice still thick with sleep. He was sitting beside her, and the twins were in the backseat.

"What was that?" said Anna, stretching as she sat up. Before Mary Ellen could answer, both Anna and Lilly were upright, peering out the windows.

She couldn't delay any longer. "We're not going to Long Beach Island," she said.

"What do you mean?" said Anna sharply. "We rented a house there. We have to go." When it came to the twins, perhaps because she was the firstborn, Anna was always the first to react.

Instead of answering directly, Mary Ellen continued quickly with her explanation. "There's been a problem at the office. I thought it best that we go someplace new, someplace no one knows about."

"What kind of problem?" asked Lilly, suddenly wide awake and, from the sound of her voice, frightened.

"If you were worried about something," said Tim, "why didn't you just call Dad?"

"Oh, please!" Anna said, shaking her head impatiently. "What would he have done? Faxed a letter to all concerned?"

"Actually, I don't think there is anything your father could have done about this," said Mary Ellen, trying to keep her voice neutral. "I'm not even sure what's going on. But just to be on the safe side, I thought it best that we get as far away as possible."

"So what are we doing here?" Lilly asked, always the practical one.

Mary Ellen briefly explained about the car exchange as she pulled up next to Heidi's car. "I'll tell you the rest later. We don't have time now."

Trading their wagon for Heidi's Grand Am was such a novelty that none of the children had a word to say until they started up again. Then Mary Ellen was in for it.

"So what's going on?" said Lilly. "Do you intend to tell us where we're going, or is that going to be your little secret?"

Mary Ellen couldn't blame her for her sarcasm. They had a right to know. Quickly and minimally, she told them about the call, about North Carolina, and even about Fitz and his boys. She tried to underplay the potential danger and slipped in the part about Fitz and his sons quickly. She wasn't sure what they would say and hoped there wouldn't be too many questions.

"We're staying with another family? That we don't know?" screeched Anna.

"I know them!" said Tim. He explained about Mike being on the team and Fitz being the coach.

"That's great," said Anna. "I'm going to share a bathroom with someone I've never laid eyes on, but it's okay because you play soccer with him!"

"You'll see, it'll be fun," Mary Ellen said. She hoped she wouldn't have a problem with their behavior. She couldn't let her children be rude at a time like this. It was, after all, Fitz's and his children's vacation as well.

"I still don't understand," said Anna. "Why are we staying with people we don't know?"

"Because it's the best choice and the only one," said Mary Ellen. She didn't blame them for being upset, but she wished they weren't so outspoken about it. But that's the way they had always been. Sometimes she wondered if she'd been too indulgent with them. If she had been stricter, would they have kept their questions and criticisms to themselves?

"What do you mean it's our only choice?" Lilly said. "We had someplace to go."

"Someone has been calling and making threats," Mary Ellen said, slowly and matter-of-factly. "Mr. Fitzpatrick offered to let us share his house with him, so that the person making the threats can't find us."

"But what does Mr. Fitzpatrick have to do with the caller? Or us?" said Anna.

"He's a policeman," she said. "And he knows about the people who are doing it." She hoped they didn't ask anything else, but to make sure, she told them they would be stopping soon at a hotel in Maryland, and then continuing on in the morning. That pleased them. They still found staying in hotels exciting, especially if there was a pool. But what really intrigued and distracted them was when she told them about Fitz's house, right on the ocean.

"I hope it's modern," said Lilly, "and has a deck overlooking the ocean."

Mary Ellen hoped it was safe.

The hotel stay went without a hitch thanks to Fitz. She realized, as she was checking in, that she couldn't pay with a credit card or check. She was just about to ask where the nearest ATM was when the receptionist explained that the room had already been paid for. Fitz must have anticipated her dilemma. She was relieved and impressed by his thoughtfulness.

By eleven the next morning they were in North Carolina, crossing over the causeway onto the Outer Banks, and entering another world. It was wild and beautiful, and just as Fitz had promised, it reminded her of Long Beach Island, with its long stretches of sand dunes and modern beach houses.

It would have been perfect if not for the uneasy feeling she'd had since she'd started driving that morning that she was being followed. There was nothing specific to explain why she thought someone was tailing them. Throughout the ride she had periodically checked her rearview mirror, but saw nothing out of the ordinary. She had changed lanes, hoping she would catch someone that way, but to no avail. Once she'd even gotten off the highway and waited to see if any of the other cars did too, but none of them had. She decided it was all in her head and forced herself to put her uneasiness aside. Besides, they were almost there. She didn't want to dampen her children's enthusiasm.

They had begun to get excited as soon as they crossed over the causeway and saw that they were really on their way to the beach. Their excitement was contagious and Mary Ellen felt the tension slip away. Still, she intended to keep a sharp eye on her children, even though the Outer Banks and Nags Head, North Carolina, seemed like a long way from New Jersey, David Anderson, and threatening phone calls.

As the children speculated about the house, she kept one eye in the rearview mirror and another eye out for a grocery store. When she saw a large supermarket just off the highway, she quickly pulled over. She'd get a good stock of food. It would be part of her contribution to their stay.

She had the children come in with her and help load up the cart. That meant more treats than she usually bought, which, she wondered, may have been her way of trying to relieve some of the guilt she felt about putting her children in jeopardy. It would not be happening if it weren't for her job and her client.

After the groceries were paid for, while the kids were stowing them in the car, she called in for her messages. First she dialed her office. Nothing there except a reminder from her secretary about her conference on the Tuesday after she got back. Then she dialed home. She listened wearily to a handful of voice mails for the twins, saving each one. Finally came the call that she had been dreading. "You may have slipped out of our reach for now, but don't be stupid enough to think you beat us," said that now-familiar voice. "We'll find you sooner or later." That was it, nothing more. She hung up, not sure what to think.

Although shaken, Mary Ellen still managed to get the children back into the car. It sounded as if whoever was after her didn't know where they were. For the time being.

Unless it was a trick. Maybe her instincts were right and they were nearby, watching their every move. She could not risk letting her children out of her sight for an instant, not until she understood what this was all about. Did Fitz know? Would he be able to tell her now who these people were and how they were involved with David? She would be glad when he was there.

As Fitz promised, the house was easy to find, right off the main road in Nags Head. What he hadn't told her was how spectacular it was. Mary Ellen was as awestruck as her children. Just as Lilly had hoped, it was ultra-modern and had all the amenities that come with a new house. There were two decks facing the ocean: one off the living room, and the other, one story above, off what she assumed was the master bedroom. There was a great room on the first floor that led into a modern kitchen, and two bedrooms and a bath on each floor. There was also a hot tub on the lower deck, which the children wanted to try immediately. They also wanted to choose their rooms.

"Let's wait until Mr. Fitzpatrick comes." She wasn't sure how she and Fitz were going to arrange things. "Leave your bags right where they are," she said, pointing to the pile of luggage in the hall. "We'll wait until they get here to decide. Instead, let's put the food away."

"What about the beach?" said Tim.

She had hoped to wait until Fitz arrived. She wondered if it was wise to risk taking them outside without Fitz. She went out on the deck and looked out over the sand and water. There were plenty of people on the beach, and she decided no one would dare try anything, not with so many witnesses. "Just as soon as we finish putting away the food," she said. It was too beautiful to be inside. But she would not let them out of her sight.

Chapter Nine

From the time that Fitz had left Mary Ellen the day before, she had not been out of his thoughts. He knew enough about the people she was up against and what they were capable of doing. He prayed the car switch and change of plans had worked to get them off her trail. To be sure, he had a Jersey state trooper follow her in an unmarked vehicle until Cape May. Then Fitz called in a few favors. Unmarked troopers from Delaware, Maryland, Virginia, and North Carolina followed her down to the beach. Each of them called in when they traded off with their counterpart, but he still didn't relax. He wanted to be there with her.

Never mind that he still didn't quite trust her. How could he, when she represented a player in a very sophisticated inter-national smuggling ring? Was it really possible that she could be that naïve to think that David Anderson was innocent? But even as little as Fitz knew about her, he didn't believe she was the kind of woman who would put her children in danger, and he honestly believed that they were.

That was why he was relieved when the alarm rang at five

thirty A.M. He had barely slept and now he could finally get on the road. It wasn't all that easy to wake up his boys, but since he'd packed the car the night before and promised them a fast-food breakfast if they were quick getting up and out, he managed to be on the road by six. From then on, except for the brief stop at McDonald's, it was a forced march south. He knew he wouldn't be comfortable until he saw with his own eyes that Mary Ellen and her children were safe.

When they reached the house, the boys excitedly rushed ahead. They were happy to be there and curious about their company. They spotted the Careys' luggage in the front hall and figured that they must have gone down to the beach. For once Fitz didn't make them unpack before heading down there. "Get into your suits and wait outside for me," he said. "I'll be right behind." He wanted to check with his office and see if they had any word on the men who were after Mary Ellen.

There was no news, so he changed, grabbed a towel, sunscreen, and his bag and followed his sons. Although the house was right on the water, there was a sand dune in front of the deck, so it was necessary to walk around it and past two houses to get onto the beach. It was the height of the season, and the beach was crowded. He was, by now, desperate to see Mary Ellen.

Even so, he forced himself to try to relax. It wouldn't do to look as worried as he felt. He didn't want to alarm his sons or Mary Ellen and her children when he finally found her. Besides, he reminded himself, he still didn't know if she was on his side.

All doubts were forgotten when he saw her. He stood on the top step of the stairs that ran down to the beach, his sons behind him, searching the crowd. It took a few minutes of scanning before he spotted her red hair peeking out from under a wide-brimmed straw hat. She was with her teenage daughters, crouched in the sand by the water, busy building a castle. Then he saw Tim a foot away, obviously sulking, with his head down, arms folded, sitting on the beach. Fitz smiled with relief. They were okay. He should have realized that she would have the sense to keep them close by her, at least until he got there. That had to be the explanation for Tim's unhappiness. She must not have let them go in the water. Smart woman!

He turned to his sons and motioned in the direction of the Careys. Then, signaling them to follow him, he quickened his pace. He knew he needed to be with her, to talk to her, to hear her voice.

He watched as she sat back, took off her hat, and sighed. She was worried, he could see that even from where he was, and he wanted to be the one to comfort her. God help him. What was happening? Right now, uppermost on his mind, was how much he would like to run right down to the shore, grab her, and hold her to him. She brought out something inside him that he thought had died a long time ago.

Mary Ellen surveyed the castle, pretending to ignore her sulking son. She'd be so glad when Fitz arrived. Then she hoped she could let them go in the water. She knew Tim was being difficult because it had been weeks since he had been able to go in the ocean. The last time they had been at the beach, his stitches had been fresh and the doctor had forbidden it. Now that the stitches were out and he could go in if she would let him, he was beside himself. His sulking was getting to her, that and the tension of the unknown.

But the castle looked good, she decided, forcing her mind back to the more mundane. It had started off as a simple cone shape, but not content, she and the girls dug out a moat and then canals leading off from there. Soon towers were added, and Mary Ellen had just started on a farm and a small village.

"Can you use a hand?"

She looked up to see Fitz standing there, smiling down at

them, his blue eyes matching the near-perfect clear sky. She jumped to her feet as she brushed the sand off her hands. "How was your trip?" she asked, suddenly feeling awkward and shy, rattled by his presence. There was no denying that she found him attractive. What a sight he was in his bathing suit, his bare shoulders and chest looking even more powerful than she remembered. Knowing she shouldn't, she stared, first at his shoulders and chest, and from there down to his flat, muscular stomach. She forced herself to turn away and face the ocean while she composed herself before she spoke.

When she turned back, she discovered him staring at her with obvious appreciation. It made her glad she had lost those ten pounds over the past year, even if the loss was because of anxiety. Anxiety, and the laps she'd been swimming at the local Y all winter to ease the tension that lately seemed to be constant.

"You finally got down here," she managed to say.

He nodded with a smile that warmed her, and then, looking from one of her daughters to the other, said, "So these are Tim's sisters, the twins."

"Anna and Lilly," she said, introducing them and beginning to feel more like herself and in control. "You'll have a hard time telling them apart at first, but if you remember that Lilly's the one with the blond streak . . ."

"That's the only difference? Really? There must be something else," he continued, looking back and forth between them.

She was happy to see how seriously he took her daughters' identities. She was also relieved to get safely around the obvious physical tension between her and Fitz by focusing on the girls. She could tell they were pleased to be noticed. But they also probably wondered about him and if there was anything between him and their mother. It was what her daughters always wondered. Before they could ask, she introduced him.

Even as she spoke, he was crouching down in the sand to see what they'd been building.

"Pretty elaborate sand castle," he said. "What's this business over here?" he asked, pointing to the canals leading off from the moat.

Lilly bent down beside him and started to explain, shyly at first, but more easily when he didn't interrupt, except to ask questions. It was Anna who first noticed Fitz's sons talking to Tim. She nudged her sister and the two went over. The boys were younger than the girls, but since they didn't have anyone close to their age, Mary Ellen knew they would make do and be friendly.

Fitz turned to Mary Ellen. "Come meet my sons," he said.

She could have picked them out in any crowd. With the same heavily lashed blue eyes and thick brown curly hair, the two boys were easily recognizable as his. She smiled as he introduced each of them.

Mike she had seen around, probably at soccer games and middle school events. But this was the first time she'd met his little brother, Robby. The two boys politely said hello, then waited a fraction of a second before asking their father if they could go in the water. Fitz turned to Mary Ellen. "What do you think?"

She shrugged. "They're desperate to. I'll leave the decision to you."

He considered. "I think they'll be okay as long as we don't let them out of our sight." He didn't add that there were two off-duty cops on the beach, buddies of his from down here, or that his service revolver was loaded and in his beach bag.

Chapter Ten

Fitz looked over at Mary Ellen and shrugged. "Well, that was easier than I expected. Hope you were finished with this castle, because I think you just lost your workers."

She grinned instead of answering, suddenly feeling tongue-tied and bashful now that they were alone. But she needed to ignore the attraction she felt. There were too many things to sort out before the children got back. It was during this awkward moment that he turned so that his back was to her, and she noticed a long scar running down his side.

"Job related," he said when he saw where she was looking.

"Pardon?" She quickly raised her eyes to his and wondered what else he could read in her face.

"The scar. I got it in Newark when I was first on the job."

"What happened?"

"Nothing exciting. Just in the wrong place at the wrong time. Got caught in some action."

The scar looked like the wound must have been deeper and more serious than his offhand response indicated. Was that because he was brave and tough, or just not ready to let her in on his feelings?

She motioned toward the water. "Do you want to join the children?"

He shook his head. "You go ahead. I think one of us should stay on shore and keep an eye on things."

She looked at him, startled. She'd almost convinced herself that things were safe. Out here in the sunshine, on the beach with him beside her, being pursued by dangerous men seemed like a dark, unreal fantasy. He obviously thought otherwise, and she hadn't even told him yet about the latest call.

"We should probably talk," she said, not sure where to begin.

"Talk?"

"Where everyone is going to sleep. Dinner. You know, make arrangements. And," she said, hesitating, "what's happening with Anderson and these phone calls."

He looked at her questioningly.

"I got another call," she blurted out.

Fitz instantly became alert and serious. "What do you mean? When did they call? Here?"

She shook her head. "They called my house, left a message. I heard it when I checked earlier today."

He grimaced and rubbed his head with one hand as if trying to wipe away the tension. "Was it the same guy?"

When she nodded, he looked at her expectantly. "What'd he say?"

She told him. "I guess it gives us breathing room," she added.

He shrugged. "Maybe. But we can't let down our guard for an instant. These guys are pros. I think you're okay right now," he continued. "But I've got someone working on a better place for your children. We need to be prepared. Best thing is if we get the children stowed away soon—someplace where they can't possibly find them."

"What about at their dad's?"

He shook his head. "That's the first place they'd look."

She couldn't imagine her children off with a stranger. And who was to say they'd be safe there?

"Don't worry," he said, reaching over and taking her hands in his. "I've done this before." He looked deeply into her eyes. "I won't let any harm come to them."

She nodded, too overwhelmed to speak.

"Ready to go on up to the house and get things squared away?" he asked, releasing her hands.

"Sure," she said. She had the feeling she'd follow him anywhere.

He signaled to the children to get out of the water. They obeyed, albeit reluctantly, and joined their parents on the sand, drying off and complaining to anyone who would listen that they were starved.

"Did you guys eat lunch? I bought lots of food and we waited for you just in case."

"We grabbed something a few hours ago, but I bet the boys would be happy to eat something now," he said, smiling. "There's nothing like having a woman around the house," he whispered, since their children were just up ahead.

"Don't get any ideas," she said, laughing. "I've already done my years of servitude."

He grinned. "It's nice for your children, though," he said almost wistfully, reminding her that his children weren't so lucky.

Chapter Eleven

When Fitz finished checking his messages on the phone in the downstairs bedroom, he headed to the kitchen. Mary Ellen had started preparing the food. When he was in sight of her, he stopped for a minute, stood back, and observed.

He liked how she had taken charge. It wasn't as if he couldn't have done it. He and his boys had been on their own for so long that all three of them were very self-sufficient. But he loved how she had brought in the feminine touch. He never would have thought of the wildflowers that she'd stuck in a pitcher and put on the table. Even paper napkins were stretching it with him. As he walked into the kitchen and checked out the food she'd laid out, he realized how simply he and his boys dined. Bologna with mustard on white bread for lunch, hamburgers and hot dogs for dinner, unless they were having pizza. He looked hungrily at the spread of food and wondered what she had planned for dinner. Even if it was hot dogs and hamburgers, he knew it would be better than what he would have served.

But it wasn't just the food. It was the warmth of a caring

woman that he'd been missing. He had watched how she treated her children, with matter-of-fact good humor, paying close attention to everything they said. He also noticed that she paid the same kind of attention to his boys. It wasn't lost on him that she'd made sure each of the children had a clean towel for their shower, including Robby and Mike.

As he listened to her singing and smelled the subtle scent of her perfume, he felt such an ache, deep inside, that he was almost frightened. He hadn't, until this very minute, realized how much he had missed living with a woman. He wondered if his boys had too.

"Finished with your calls?" she asked, turning to him. He nodded. They were going to have to talk about those calls, but seeing her now standing there in the kitchen, a look of contentment on her face, made him decide to postpone that conversation. Instead, since the kids were still showering, he asked her if she wanted to see the rest of the house.

Mary Ellen pointed to the pile of luggage by the front door. "I told the kids not to put their bags in any of the rooms," she said. "Where do you want us?"

"Why don't you and the girls take the upstairs bedrooms? Tim can bunk with Robby and Mike."

When she agreed, he grabbed the girls' two bags in one hand, her bag in the other, and nodded in the direction of the stairs.

"I hope we're not imposing," she said, feeling like a helpless damsel as she watched him put the girls' bags in the first room they came to. "This is your vacation. How do your boys feel about us intruding like this?"

"They're fine about it. To them it's always a treat to have another family along, especially if there's a mother in the picture. My sons are a bit like Peter Pan's Lost Boys," he explained. "They welcome the chance to be around a mom. You have no idea how much they are going to appreciate your cooking." He walked into the room that was to be hers and, after putting her bag down, went out onto the deck. She followed, taking in the smell of the ocean and listening to the waves breaking. If only this were a real vacation.

"You've got a great view from here," he said as he took her hand and drew her over to where he was standing so she could see the full line of the coast. "You can see miles down the beach."

There was nothing in his voice or manner to indicate he wanted anything more than to show her the shoreline. Maybe she was the only one who felt the attraction. There was no denying that she did. As she stepped next to him, she could feel her heart beat faster. Even when he pulled her nearer so she could see more of the view, his manner was calm, as if it was no big deal to be standing so close. But it was all she could do to control her racing heart and mask the tension she was feeling. He betrayed none, continuing to talk, one hand resting on her shoulder, as he pointed down the coast.

"If you follow the line of the beach," he said, his voice low and easy, "you can see for almost two miles. One day this week we'll drive down that way and I'll show you. Sometimes you can see even farther," he added, "almost down to Cape Hatteras. At least that's what the boys and I like to think."

She listened to his words while she tried not to be so aware of him. She didn't trust her feelings. It had been so long. She wasn't sure what she felt or what to do about it. She could smell the suntan lotion still on his skin, and see every freckle that had come out with the afternoon sun. There seemed to be a warm glow flowing between them, and she thought she caught a questioning look of desire when their eyes accidentally met. But she might have been mistaken, for when she looked again, trying to read his thoughts, his eyes gave nothing away and she was left to wonder. Did he feel it too, or was it all one-sided?

"Well," Fitz said, suddenly letting go of her arm. "It sounds like the children are finished with their showers."

She nodded, for she too could hear them chattering excitedly and the sounds of their footsteps below.

He looked at her and raised his eyebrows. "Guess we'd better go on down and eat," he added with a sheepish grin, dropping the arm that had been resting on her shoulder.

She couldn't ignore what she was feeling. Even when they were all together in the kitchen eating their sandwiches, she was conscious of him. As she poured lemonade for each of the children, she was aware of how good he looked standing there in his bathing suit and T-shirt, his hair brushed back off his face.

What would it be like, she wondered, to run her hands over those powerful shoulders and feel his full lips on hers? She pushed the thought out of her mind, aware of how crazy it was. She was hiding out from dangerous men who wanted to harm her children. It was not the time to be attracted to her protector. She had to get a grip before she did something foolish.

Perhaps it was fortunate that, although they were together for the rest of the day, Fitz and Mary Ellen were never alone. They spent the afternoon on the beach, but took turns going in the water with the children so one of them could be on land in case there was a problem.

As she expected, the children were having a great time. Tim was happy to have other boys to play with and the twins were glad for a chance to work on their tans. They were also bowled over by the house, with its deck and built-in hot tub. But it wasn't the house that the girls talked about when they flopped down on beach chairs beside her.

"Mr. Fitzpatrick is nice. Don't you think so, Mom?" said Lilly, exchanging a meaningful look with Anna.

"I think he's hot," said Anna. She was the child who always pushed the limits.

"I don't like you using that expression," Mary Ellen said automatically.

"Everyone does. Besides, he is, especially with that scar. It makes him look like a gangster."

"He got it in the line of duty," said Mary Ellen, hoping the truth would squash her daughter's romantic imagination.

"Wow! Imagine Mom with a boyfriend who's been shot!"

"He's not a boyfriend. He's Tim's friend's father, his coach, and a policeman who is helping us. I told you that."

"Maybe," said Anna, "but he doesn't act like that. I mean, he *did* put his arm around you." She grinned at her sister. "We saw."

"I am telling you, he's not my boyfriend, so get it out of your heads."

"Whatever," said Anna. "We won't say another word."

"I would appreciate it," Mary Ellen answered, holding on to the last shred of her dignity. She resolved that from now on nothing between her and Fitz would give the children anything to think about.

For the rest of the afternoon there was so little contact between them that even she'd begun to doubt the feelings she'd had earlier. By evening, all she was sure of was a growing friendship between the two families.

Mary Ellen had bought chicken for Fitz to grill. She was putting together a simple pasta salad to go with it when Fitz went to his room to make some calls. When he returned to the kitchen ten minutes later, she looked at him expectantly. Maybe he had some news.

"We're trying to find the safest place for your kids," he said.

The children were all in the hot tub, out of earshot, so they could talk freely. Mary Ellen needed to know what was happening, but she wanted to keep it to a minimum so they wouldn't worry unnecessarily. "We're also watching the people we think are involved with Anderson," he added.

"But if you know who's involved—"

He shook his head before she finished the sentence. "We don't have proof. That's what we're hoping to get from David. But," he said, before she could reply, "that's another story, one which I've no authority to discuss. What I *can* do is talk about where to send the children."

"I wish they could stay with me."

"I know," he said, "but it's too risky. At the moment we're thinking New England. That's probably far enough away. I'll know more later in the week. In the meantime," he said, putting his hands on her shoulders and looking at her with intensity, "let's try to enjoy the time we have here."

He had a point, and when he suggested that they get up at seven the following morning to go crabbing, she quickly agreed. The hour seemed ungodly for people on vacation, but Fitz explained that early morning was when the crabs were biting.

She still had to get through the night, which, she discovered, was not such an easy feat. She was worried about leaving her children. She hated the idea that they would not be with her, but would be staying with someone she didn't even know. It was in their best interest, for their safety, that they go to a safe house, but that didn't ease her pain.

She lay in bed thinking about where they might be going and trying to come up with a comforting way to break the news to them. But that wasn't all that was keeping her awake. Although she and the girls were sleeping on a different floor from Fitz and the boys, they were still in the same house. She had a hard time settling down knowing he was under the same roof and also awake. She could hear the soft sounds of jazz coming from the first floor and occasional footsteps. At one point, when she was sure that it was Fitz walking around, she almost went down to talk to him. She rationalized that since they both were awake . . . Fortunately, sense intruded and she stayed where she was.

Morning did finally come, and shortly before seven, the two families, barely awake, drove down to the causeway to rent crab boats. Fitz took the twins and she went with the boys, since they claimed to know what they were doing. For about an hour, they all puttered around the bay collecting crabs.

The boys were easy enough to be with, but they were busy pulling in their bounty and didn't do much talking. Looking over to the other boat, Mary Ellen could see that Lilly and Anna were chewing Fitz's ear off. She wished she could hear what they were saying, but the boys started to get restless, particularly after their buckets were full.

"Can I steer the boat?" asked Tim.

"Sure," she said, and then looked over at the other two boys. "You guys want to?"

They nodded, really smiling for the first time that day, probably because they were finally waking up.

"Just be careful," she said as she changed places with Tim, "that you don't capsize the boat. First rule of boating is keeping the weight even!"

"Mom! You worry too much!" said Tim. "Look how shallow it is here." Which of course was the reason Mary Ellen had no qualms about letting any of them handle the small dinghy with its low-powered engine. The whole scene brought back wonderful memories of her days at the shore in the marshes and bays of Long Beach Island, and she wanted them to have some of those memories too.

Tim was more adventurous than Mary Ellen had been and

soon had them traveling along the shore at a good clip. They left Fitz and the girls behind. Mary Ellen sat back and enjoyed the ride. It wasn't as if they could get lost, and they all could swim, so there was no reason why they had to keep Fitz in sight. At least that's what she figured, until she realized that a boat had been circling them for some time. After the third pass, she began to wonder whether they needed assistance. It seemed unlikely that David's friends had already found them. Would they really track them out in the bay? Even so, she decided they had to get back to Fitz.

By now Mike was skippering. "Turn around," she ordered. "We're going back." When all three boys looked at her, startled, she realized that her words had come out more sharply than she'd intended. She made an effort to sound more relaxed as she explained, "Your dad's going to wonder where we are."

None of them looked convinced, but Mary Ellen was firm. Although the motorboat was too far away for her to read the lettering on its side, much less make out its occupants, it was fast approaching. It occurred to her that in their wooden dinghy, they were sitting ducks.

But it wasn't as easy to get back. When they turned the dinghy around, both the tide and the wind were against them. Besides, their boat wasn't powerful and was straining against the current. Progress was slow. Meanwhile, the motorboat continued to approach.

"Mrs. Carey, cut the engine. We are coming alongside," hollered someone through a bullhorn. She still couldn't make out who was aboard the boat.

"Cut the engine!"

Chapter Twelve

Mary Ellen stared at the approaching boat, frozen with fear. It made a sharp angle to the side and she was able to make out the lettering on its bow: MARINE PATROL.

Thank God! Whatever they wanted, it wasn't to hurt her children. She breathed easily for the first time since its approach.

As the boat came closer, she was able to make out the passengers standing on the bow: Fitz, Anna, and Lilly. What the heck were they doing there? Had Fitz's boat capsized? Was there news she needed to know right away? She waited anxiously as the boat came closer.

In minutes the boat was upon them, its wake causing their small dinghy to rock back and forth. As Fitz stood and watched, the Marine Patrol officer pulled alongside and threw her a line. "Having any problems?" he shouted over the engine's noise.

"No, we were just cruising. Is something wrong?" She looked from him to Fitz, trying to read the answer in their faces.

The officer shook his head. "Looked like you were having a rough time getting back," he said. "Throw me a line and let me tow you. No reason to get your husband and kids all riled up," he added, under his breath.

She glanced over at Fitz, who still didn't speak. She threw the officer a line. Although she wondered what Fitz must have told him, she was grateful for the assistance. With the tide being the way it was, it had been harder getting back than she'd expected, but she didn't understand why Fitz thought he needed to rescue her. He still stood mute, his arms folded across his chest, shaking his head.

"Mom, you okay?" shouted Lilly over the engines.

Mary Ellen nodded.

"We were worried about you. Why did you let the boys take you out of sight?" said Anna.

So that was the problem. Mary Ellen turned and looked at Fitz, who continued to shake his head. She was starting to feel silly and didn't like that one bit. That's what happened when you got involved with a man.

"What exactly were you thinking?" said Fitz. "I was beside myself with worry."

They were back at the house and finally alone, upstairs on the deck outside her room. This was their first opportunity to discuss that morning's incident. The kids were all downstairs cleaning up after lunch.

She sighed. "Can you just stop?"

"Seriously—"

"You're just looking for another opportunity to make me feel bad. I've already acknowledged that I shouldn't have let the boys take the boat out of your sight. Maybe it was reckless. But don't you think you pushed the panic button a little prematurely, or were you just trying to let me know who's boss? And by the way, what was that business about me being your wife?"

He had the good grace to look embarrassed. "It seemed easier to say that than to explain the whole relationship. The girls got a kick out of it," he said, smiling for the first time.

She raised her eyebrows, but did not give him the satisfaction of a smile, although she was tempted. He looked so good right now that instead of arguing with him, she wanted to be in his arms. But that would have been unseemly. She didn't want to back down, even though she was beginning to realize he might have a point.

He made the first concession.

"Maybe I was being overprotective, and I probably shouldn't have said you were my wife, though I don't see what the big deal is, but you've got to be more careful! You're dealing with dangerous people here! You had *my* sons and you disappeared for half an hour. You don't know the area or the tides, and I don't know what kind of sailor you are. I had reason to worry."

"Perhaps, but the Marine Patrol?"

Instead of answering, he just shook his head.

"I get your point. I'll be more careful," she said. "And I'll trust you to figure out the safest place for my children to hide. But it doesn't do anyone any good to go on about it the way you are!"

He grinned sheepishly. "You're right. I was worried. I won't mention it again. Let's go enjoy the beach," he said, extending his hand. "We don't know how much longer we'll have down here."

Hours later, the morning's misunderstanding long forgotten, they sat down for their crab dinner out on the deck. She could not remember ever having a better time at the beach, and she didn't want it to end.

"Like this?" asked Tim, slamming the hammer down on the crab shell in front of him. "It's really okay?" He was sitting between Robby and Mike, who was next to Fitz.

"Yeah," Fitz said with a smile. "That's how you do it. Now just scoop out the meat with your fingers."

"Your fingers?" said Anna, looking across from where she was sitting beside her mother. Fitz nodded and demonstrated with the crab before him.

They were gathered around the picnic table overlooking the ocean. The children had set the table with paper towels and plastic utensils and used newspapers for a tablecloth, as was the tradition, according to Fitz. Mary Ellen had put every candle and lantern she could find on the deck so they'd be able to see their food as the light faded.

"Good thing we have all these paper towels," said Lilly, "or Mom would have a fit."

Mary Ellen looked up and smiled, catching Robby's eye as he was about to wipe his hands on his shirt. Thinking better of it, he reached across Tim for one of the paper towels. She was as contented as she'd ever been and saw that contentment reflected in the tanned faces of her children as she looked around the table. That feeling quickly vanished when she came to Fitz. The look he exchanged with her was far from content, and instead bespoke promises of yearning and passion. She looked away, but not before he ignited needs deep within her that she hadn't known still existed. Frightened and unsure if she had misunderstood, she tried to catch her breath and hide her feelings.

"Have some more," she said, extending the plate of crabs in his direction.

He looked at her and smiled gently, signs of passion gone. "I'm all set. But thanks for thinking of me. You're being awfully sweet," he added, leaning closer to her and speaking softly. "Does that mean you're getting past the Marine Patrol business?"

"Maybe, or perhaps it's that the salt air has mellowed me out," she said. "You'll see when we get back. I'll be the same old crab."

"At least you know yourself," said Tim, as the others hooted.

"Pipe down, you guys," said Fitz. "If you're finished," he continued, speaking to all five children, "start clearing the table. Mary Ellen and I are going for a walk."

"Whoa!" said Mike. "Dad wants to be alone with your mom!"

"Michael!" said his father, suddenly serious. "Mind your manners!" He grabbed his and Mary Ellen's glass and the half-empty bottle of chardonnay and signaled for her to follow him down the steps, toward the beach. She knew he wanted to talk about what plans were in the works for the children. He had assured her that two off-duty cops who were friends of his from Nags Head would be watching the house and keeping an eye on the kids.

She marveled at how he'd maneuvered their escape. Instead of arguing or discussing what their parents were up to, the children were actually cleaning up. Mary Ellen would have liked to reach over and hug him. It was great to share the responsibilities of child rearing even for just a few days. They walked in silence. The soft ocean breeze cooled down the temperature on the beach. Mary Ellen listened to waves crashing on the shore and watched the pink sky slowly fade. It had been just about a perfect day. She sighed, afraid to hope it would last.

"Shall we?" he asked, indicating a spot to sit just above the high tide mark.

"Mmm," she said, following his lead. They sat there for a while, side by side, sipping their wine, watching the waves crash on the beach.

"It looks like we'll be leaving tomorrow," Fitz said suddenly.

"What?" She felt a sharp dull pain in the pit of her stomach. What she had been dreading was finally going to happen. Her contentment was quickly replaced with a sense of doom. "Why so soon?"

"We don't think we can trust these guys to leave you alone much longer. We want your children safely away before there is any risk."

She understood. But she couldn't bear the thought of being separated from them even if she knew she had no choice. She shuddered involuntarily. She must be brave and face what was ahead. Wrapping her arms around herself, she turned to him, trying to keep her voice firm. "What's the plan?"

He reached over and pulled her closer to him, resting his arm on her shoulder as he spoke. "It's still not totally ironed out. What's certain is that we will be driving up to the airport in Norfolk tomorrow. We'll meet up with my men there who will escort your children to the safe house."

The concrete details forced her to believe that it was really going to happen. "This is going to be very difficult," she whispered.

"I know," he said, squeezing her shoulder and pulling her even closer. "I wish there was something I could do to make it easier for you. I can only promise that I will be here for you and that I will see to it that your children are completely protected. You're not in this alone."

She believed him, especially when he took her in his arms and brought her closer to him. She was grateful that he didn't patronize her and say that there was nothing to worry about. They both knew that wasn't true. Instead, he just held her tightly and slowly rocked her back and forth. She was certain that he understood what she was going through, that he cared about her and her children and would do all he could to keep them safe.

She leaned back, wanting to look at him. With only the moon for light, she was barely able to make out even the outlines of his face, which made her more aware of the roughness of his beard and the silkiness of his hair.

"I wish none of this was happening. We are going to do our

best to protect you all, but I wish to God you and your children had nothing to do with these people," he said, stroking her hair. More than words could ever do, his soft, gentle strokes managed to soothe her troubled soul. She settled down into his arms and without thinking reached up and ran her fingers through his thick curls. When he sighed, she snuggled closer. It felt so good to be with him. She'd been alone and isolated for so long.

Then, as if it were the most natural thing in the world, her mouth found his. When their lips touched, she closed her eyes and cautiously returned his first tentative kiss, suddenly feeling as if she were finally home.

When she responded, his kiss became deeper and more demanding. But instead of making her afraid, she only felt a deep yearning confirming how much she wanted him.

"Ever since I laid eyes on you," Fitz murmured, "I've been wanting to do this." He pulled her closer and wrapped his arms tightly around her. He lifted up her mouth to his and kissed her again. She stopped thinking and gave in to the rich feelings being stirred up, feelings that had been dormant for some time. Encircling his neck with her arms, she returned his kisses as he crushed her hair in his hands and softly murmured her name.

His kisses, although deep, were also slow and easy enough to make her feel as if his only wish was to taste her lips and hold her in his arms. Although they churned up her insides and wakened longings she desperately wanted fulfilled, the kisses also soothed, as if he had all the time in the world to please her.

But they didn't have that kind of time—not now. She knew their children would be waiting. "The kids," she reluctantly reminded him between kisses.

He groaned as he let her go. "They're probably timing us," he said with a sigh.

She giggled. "And imagining and discussing what might be going on."

"I'm sure you're right," he said, helping her get to her feet.

"We've all had such a good time down here," she said, suddenly feeling shy in the aftermath of their new intimacy. "Even though it's only been a few days, I know that none of us are going to forget it."

"Me too," he said. He reached over and smoothed back her hair, gently tucking a few loose strands behind her ears. "Today was fun, even if you had to get towed in by the Marine Patrol."

She reached up and put her hand over his mouth to muffle him. "You promised!"

"Agreed," he said after taking her hand and pushing it aside so he could speak, but not before he kissed each finger.

She enjoyed the sensation and remained close even when his hands found her waist and pulled her toward him. It was only after he kissed her again that she gently pushed him away. "We should get back."

"You're right. But I promise you," he said, his voice suddenly gruff, "when this is all over, you and I are going to take all the time we need to get to know one another properly." Then he leaned down and rubbed his lips against hers as if sealing his promise.

She smiled in the darkness, trying to ignore the power this man already had over her—able to so easily change her moods with his words. As they got closer to the house, Mary Ellen began to see circles of light emanating from it. She tried not to panic. "Do you see that?" she said, pointing. Before he had a chance to answer, she discovered the source of the lights: their children. Armed with the flashlights she had found in her search for lanterns and candles, they were circling the area in front of the house. As soon as she and Fitz got within tracking distance, a glare blinded Mary Ellen.

"I found them," squealed Robby.

Immediately, five beams focused on her and Fitz, greeting the two of them like long-lost voyagers and providing a lighted path for their journey back to the house.

She was embarrassed to be the object of their search, and didn't feel any better when they were inside the house, gathered in the kitchen, as Fitz scooped out ice cream for their dessert. It was impossible to miss her daughters' exchange of knowing glances or Mike's and Tim's smirks. Maybe Robby was the only one who didn't recognize the beginning signs of romance.

It was the first time the children had ever seen her with anyone other than their father. She had to expect they'd have some reaction. It was a reminder that she couldn't forget about their sensibilities.

"Some for you?" said Fitz as his hand hovered over the dessert bowl in front of her.

She shook her head. She felt too stirred up to eat.

"Coffee then?" he asked.

She nodded. "As long as it's decaf. It's just about time for bed. Nearly ten," she added after looking at her watch in surprise. The evening had gone so fast.

"Can we sleep out on the deck?" asked Tim, at the same time that Mike asked his father.

Before she had a chance to answer, Fitz did. "Not tonight."

"But you always let us," protested Mike.

Mary Ellen was relieved when Fitz countered with an alternate plan. "You can have a sleepover downstairs in the family room."

"Really? And watch a movie?"

"I think so," said Fitz, glancing over at Mary Ellen to see what she thought.

Before she could say anything, Anna was on her. "Us too?"

She hesitated. "Only if you behave yourselves—"

"Oh, Mom!" interrupted Anna. "What do you think will happen?"

Mary Ellen shook her head and looked over at Fitz to see what he thought. As usual, when Lilly wanted something, she could be very persuasive.

He was watching them intently, a smile on his face, obviously enjoying the interaction. "It's okay by me. But that doesn't mean it's an excuse for an all-night pajama party!" he said, suddenly looking sternly at each child. "And no scary movies! Remember the boys are younger than you," he warned in a voice that would have convinced her he meant it, except for the betraying twinkle in his eye.

While Mary Ellen settled the kids in the basement, Fitz was busy on the phone. He was still at it when she came inside. She was almost relieved. Sharing a house with him last night had been awkward enough. Now that the memory of his kisses still burned and she knew with certainty that the attraction she felt for him was returned, bidding him good night would be doubly difficult. Quickly, before he got off the phone, she went up to her room.

She was there, sitting out on the deck, when there was a soft knock on her door.

Fitz was so exhausted, from lack of sleep and the strain of worrying about this woman and her children, that he almost couldn't think straight. But he wanted to let her know what the plans were for the morning. Although he hated to have to tell her about the danger they might be facing, he thought she would be more cautious and more accepting if she knew exactly what was happening. Besides, he was desperate to see her. He had hardly slept the night before thinking about her lying in bed on the floor above him. Now that he knew she returned his interest, there was nothing that would stop him from at least dropping by.

But when she delayed in answering his knock, finally appearing with her blanket around her, he wasn't so sure it had been such a good idea. She hadn't been expecting him; that was clear.

"Did I wake you?" he mumbled awkwardly.

When she shook her head he forced himself to ask, "Can I come in, just for a minute?"

She perched at the edge of the bed, draping the blanket around her, and motioned for him to sit on the rocker across from her.

"I just got off the phone with my contacts in New England," he said, after sitting down in the chair. "Do you want to hear what we've planned? Is it too late?" He suddenly felt shy and a little stupid. Was it wrong for him to have come up here? It had been so long since he'd been with a woman like her that he wasn't clear about the rules anymore.

"It's fine," she whispered. With her arms folded over the blanket, across her chest, and her legs crossed in front of her, she didn't look so sure. "Tell me what's happening."

Mary Ellen sat quietly as Fitz looked off into space, as if planning what he would say. When he finally did speak, it was softly and slowly, as if he was measuring every word. "First of all, you should know that they've tracked these guys—the ones we think are after you—as far as the Maryland shore. Then we lost them. We're not sure if they're down as far as North Carolina, or if they lost your trail and are wandering around up in Maryland. But," he added quickly, "we can't take any chances. The safest thing is to move out of here tomorrow."

She nodded, taking in what he'd said. They were safe now, but whoever was after them could find them anytime. It would be best if they could hide the kids while it was clear. Her family's safety was the most important thing.

Fitz filled her in on the logistics, explaining how they would drive in two cars to the Norfolk airport. "Then you will drive back to Maplewood with me and the boys in my car. We figure that should put off anyone who might be looking for you."

She shook her head but didn't say anything right away. She was thinking about what they'd planned. She pushed aside trivial worries such as what her children would wear; all their clothes were at home except for a few beach things. She tried not to think about where they would go to school. They could figure that out later. "Do you know where the children will be staying? Who will be taking care of them?"

"No. You won't either. Another precaution," he explained when she started to object. "No one can get to you or me and find out."

She wrapped her arms even more tightly around herself and sighed. The plan made sense. She could see that. But these were her children they were talking about. She wouldn't even know where they were! "Will they be in good hands?" she asked. "They may seem grown up, but they are my babies. Promise me you'll take care of them and won't let anything happen to them."

Fitz wished there was something he could say to reassure her. He rued the day she ever got involved. It wasn't right that her family was in this kind of danger, but there was nothing he could do. He gazed at her, trying to find the right words. When she looked back at him and he saw her face start to crumble, he forgot everything he'd promised himself before he entered her room. He got up and went to her. Sitting down beside her, he put his arms around her and gently stroked her hair. "They'll be home before you know it," he murmured.

"Is that really true? With all the adjournments and delays, the trial could go on for months," she said, her voice muffled because he'd pressed her against his chest. She leaned back and looked up at him. "I know it's the only way, but I just hate the idea of them staying with someone I don't even know. What if the person doesn't understand them? What if they get scared? Who's going to explain what's happening? I just wish—" She sighed. "It's not that I don't appreciate—"

"You don't have to say anything," he said softly. "I'd feel the same. I wish we didn't have to do this, but it's the only way."

She leaned her head against his chest, her arms tightly around him. "I can't imagine what it will be like. I'll miss them," she added softly, tempted to check on them that very minute, while they were still with her.

He nodded with understanding. "Of course you will. But I promise they'll be safe," he said. "This is the only way we can be sure of that," he added.

She looked up when he spoke and was about to respond when he leaned down and gently kissed her lips. She hadn't been expecting that, had been in his arms only for comfort, but when he started kissing her, she automatically responded and then, as the kisses deepened and passion flared, she found herself getting lost in the feelings that had been steadily growing since they met.

She'd felt so alone. Now she had the comfort of his kisses and the security of his arms, but there was also something more that she couldn't deny. His kisses were awakening feelings that had been hidden for too long.

It was when he gathered her up so that he could lie beside her that she came to her senses. It was only then that she stopped and thought about what was happening between them.

"This isn't the time," she said, sitting up straight and gently pushing him away. "We can't do this. Not now."

At her words, his hands stopped moving over her. He looked

up and shook his head, as if awakening from a trance. "Sorry," he said, after collecting himself. "My fault. Didn't mean to. Just suddenly—"

She nodded. "It wasn't just you. I don't know what came over me. But the kids—"

"They're busy with their movies, I'm sure. But," he said, almost sheepishly, "you don't have to explain. I understand."

She smiled with relief.

"We should both be getting to bed," she said awkwardly, "and getting some sleep." Her head was clear now, and she could do what she had to, but even so, it was with great regret that she let him slip out of her room. As she lay in her lonely bed afterward, she thought of him only one floor away. What if, she wondered, they never got the chance? She knew now was not the time. She hoped there would one day be a time, when all this was over and the children were out of danger, that they could be together. She was sure that Fitz was the kind of man she had been searching for, someone she and her children could count on and someone she could love.

Chapter Thirteen

I still don't understand why we can't stay with you," said Anna. She was sitting in the front seat next to Mary Ellen. It was her turn to ride shotgun. "If we're in danger, why aren't you?"

Mary Ellen didn't say anything for a minute. She was focused on keeping up with Fitz, who was in front of her on the highway. They had been on the road for an hour and had another hour to go before they would reach the Norfolk airport. Even though she knew there were several policemen in unmarked cars also on the road, she did not want to let Fitz out of her sight.

"Anna, before we left home, a man called my office and threatened to hurt the three of you. He didn't say anything about me."

The three children were silent. They had not been happy to have their vacation end so abruptly. They must have seen how serious she and Fitz were about leaving this morning, and maybe because they were overtired from staying up so late the night before, they didn't protest too much when she first told them what was happening. But now that they were waking up, it seemed to be hitting them.

"Why can't we just stay at Dad's?" asked Tim. "Is it because you're still mad at him?"

She sighed. If only it were that easy. "No, honey. This has nothing to do with your dad. In fact, I wish you *were* staying with him, but Mr. Fitzpatrick believes that is the first place anyone would look for you. We don't want to take any chances, so you are going to a safe house that no one knows about."

"Not even you?" asked Lilly in a small voice.

"It's better that I don't know where you will be. But it's not as if no one knows." Mary Ellen did her best not to let her voice catch and betray her fears. "The police and the FBI do. If there is something you need to tell me or if I have to get ahold of you, we can do it through them. Okay?"

"The FBI? Really?"

"Really." She thought Tim might find the FBI's involvement exciting. She hoped it would be exciting enough to distract him, particularly when the going got tough.

"Can we call you if we have something important to tell you?" asked Anna.

Mary Ellen sighed. This was so difficult for all of them, and the idea of the FBI being involved would not be a distraction for her daughters. "I'm afraid not. The FBI and the police are concerned that I will be watched and that my phone will be tapped. We don't want to take chances or give away your whereabouts."

"Couldn't we e-mail you?" asked Tim.

"What do you mean?" she asked.

"I bet the FBI has a Web site. Why can't we e-mail you through the FBI?"

"Maybe," she said. The world of computers continued to intimidate her. Her children had a much better understanding of it. "Why don't we ask them when we get to the airport?"

They drove in silence for so long that Mary Ellen began to think the children had fallen asleep. Then she looked in the rearview mirror and saw Tim and Lilly huddled together, their arms around each other. She thought she would break down. For those two adversaries to band together, they had to be in great fear of what was out there.

Once they reached the airport, things moved very quickly. She followed Fitz to a private, highly secure parking area, where they were escorted by several men in dark suits to an unmarked terminal. Mary Ellen stood back and watched, her arms around her three children, as Fitz dealt with the men. Suddenly, the slightly older man who appeared to be in charge emerged from the group and approached Mary Ellen. He extended his hand in greeting.

"Joe Murphy, FBI," he said, meeting her eyes. He motioned for her to step away with him, probably so they could talk privately. "I know this is very difficult for you," he said quietly. "Believe me when I say that they will be in good hands. Most of us are parents ourselves and are doing our best to make sure they will be in a secure situation."

She nodded, unable to speak, afraid she would cry. That would be unthinkable—at least in front of her children.

"We're ready to move them out," he said. "Do you want to say your good-byes?"

She nodded and turned to the three, who looked as vulnerable as preschoolers being left on the first day of nursery school—only this wasn't nursery school and it wouldn't be for a few hours. "It's only for a short while," she said as she gathered her children into her arms. "Please be brave and promise me you will be kind to each other. At least you'll be together. If you can remember to take care of one another, you'll be okay."

When each solemnly nodded, she thought they were going to get through this parting in one piece. But when a single tear trickled down Lilly's cheek, it was too much.

"I don't know why we have to go," cried Anna. "What if something happens to you? Then what will we do? Will we have to live with Dad?"

"I don't want to leave you alone," said Tim. "You shouldn't be in that house all by yourself."

Lilly didn't say anything because she was crying too hard.

Mary Ellen dropped her arms from around them and spoke firmly. "Nothing's going to happen to me. I've got a job to do and Mr. Fitzpatrick will be there if I need any help. You know I wouldn't let you go if I had any choice. This is the only way to keep you safe."

Anna started to speak, but before she could, Mary Ellen continued quickly. "The man is waiting for you to get on that plane," she said, motioning toward the plane that awaited them. "Do as he says and I promise you this will all be over soon. Before you know it, we'll all be back together."

The next morning, back in New Jersey and in her office, Mary Ellen tried to come to terms with what had happened. Uprooting her children and not knowing where they were or who they were with was so painful, but she was trying her best not to think about it. She needed to get out of this case so they could be reunited.

As soon as she arrived at the office, she began preparing an affidavit requesting that she be removed as David's counsel.

But getting out of the case wasn't going to be that easy. When she called the judge's chambers and told his clerk what she wanted, the clerk reminded Mary Ellen that she would need her client's permission. That's what she was waiting for now—to talk to David. She'd called his apartment earlier, but his roommate said he wasn't in. She'd left a message.

The phone rang now and she snatched it up, hoping it would be David. But her heart sank when she heard his father's voice instead.

"Mary Ellen," Kirk Anderson began, "what seems to be the problem? I understand you were looking for David. I thought you were still on vacation. I hope you didn't come back for our benefit. We try not to be demanding clients."

She suppressed her impatience. He was going to make this so difficult. "It's David I'm looking for," she said, forcing a tone of congeniality, but hoping she sounded determined. She couldn't let him manipulate her like he did everybody else. Too much depended on her holding her own.

"David's away," said Anderson. "Went down to the shore for a few days."

"He's not supposed to leave the area. Doing so could mean he forfeits his bail," she said, dismayed.

Anderson was dismissive. "He didn't leave New Jersey. He only went down to the shore. Besides, who would tell them? Certainly not his own lawyer!"

"Of course not, it's just that—"

"Let me do the worrying," said Anderson. "You deal with getting him off."

"Well, actually, that's why I was calling," she said. "I want to talk to David about changing attorneys." She waited for the explosion. She didn't have to wait long.

"What are you saying? You can't do that!"

"I've got to," said Mary Ellen. "My children have been threatened. I've been threatened. I can't put them in danger, not even for you."

"Threats? Phone calls? Why didn't you call me earlier?" he said, his voice suddenly softening and sounding concerned, almost fatherly. "Why didn't you come to me?"

"I didn't want to bother you," she said, knowing how lame that sounded. Go to him? At this point she was afraid to trust *anyone,* including Kirk Anderson. For all she knew, he could be behind the phone calls. She wouldn't go to him. Not in a million years, not if her life depended on it, which might even be the case.

"You're never a bother," said Anderson, almost soothingly. "You know how much David's mother and I appreciate all you've done for him. Which is why you can't let him down now. He trusts you. He needs you!"

She did not respond.

"Have you gone to the police?" he asked. "A nice woman like you with a family shouldn't have to put up with those kinds of threats! There must be something they can do!"

"I was in touch with the police," she said, "but they couldn't stop the calls—not until they have more to go on, so I had to send my children away. I've got to get off this case." She didn't mention Fitz. Anderson didn't need to know everything.

"I understand your worry," he said, "but David is my son, and, like you, I am a concerned parent. Let me make a few calls. Maybe I can find out what's going on. But you must represent David. He's my son, Mary Ellen. I can't let you off the case. Understand? I have to look out for him."

After she hung up, she stared at the phone and wondered what to do. She didn't want to lose her job. She needed the money. But if she continued to represent David, she couldn't stay here. If only Dunphy were here, she could go in and talk to him. He'd help her get a read on Anderson and the possible repercussions of not complying with his request. His secretary had said he did not want to be disturbed unless it was a life or death matter. Would this qualify?

The phone rang again. This time it was Fitz.

"We need to talk," he said. "Can I come up to your office? I'm just downstairs."

Chapter Fourteen

Is this about the children? Are they all right?" Mary Ellen tried to keep the panic that she felt out of her voice, but she knew she wasn't succeeding.

"The children are okay," Fitz said. "Someone spoke to them this morning and said they were adjusting nicely. He asked me to tell you that you have good kids. He's sure they'll do just fine. But that's not the only reason I'm calling."

"Of course, come up. I'm on the ninth floor."

While she waited, she thought about the ride up from North Carolina. One of Fitz's people had driven Heidi's car and she'd ridden with Fitz and his sons. They'd driven straight up, only stopping for gas and to pick up food. Fitz did most of the driving, but periodically he'd asked Mary Ellen to take over so he could rest.

A couple of times when she was driving, he fell asleep. Once he even rested his head on her shoulder, and she'd liked that—liked that he was relying on her. But what she remembered most about the trip were the conversations.

The first conversation was with the boys. They were in the

backseat. She was worried they would be angry about their vacation being cut short, but Fitz must have explained some of what was going on. When she got into the car after seeing her children off, both Robby and Mike had looked at her solemnly, as if they understood how she felt. Then Robby spoke.

"Dad says they'll only be gone for a little while."

She nodded, unsure if she was capable of speaking without breaking down. Perhaps he sensed that, for he was quiet for a moment. Then he reached over the seat, touched her cheek, and softly said, "It's okay to cry. We understand."

She nodded, and, as if she had been waiting for permission, the tears began to flow. No one in the car spoke as she silently wept, although Fitz reached over and squeezed her hand. Because of that and Robby's words, she felt much less alone. She even began to feel better. Her children wouldn't be gone forever, and they were safer away from her. Now she just needed to get off this case so they could come home.

She must have dozed off after that. When she woke they were in Maryland, driving along its eastern shore. She looked over at Fitz, who put his index finger to his lips and then pointed to the backseat. Both boys had dropped off to sleep.

Fitz pulled off the road at the next service station, filled up the tank, and picked up containers of coffee for them both. Then, when they were back on the highway, he started to talk.

First they talked about the soccer team, what he thought of Tim's abilities, and how he thought the team would help his lack of confidence.

"That's one of the reasons I wanted him to play," she said. "Even when we were married, his dad never had a lot of time for him. Work and his own interests always came first. Now that there are just the girls and me, I figure Tim needs some men in his life. Playing soccer seemed like the best opportunity to fix that."

"A little male guidance and companionship?"

She nodded. "Do you think that's silly?"

He shook his head. "Not at all. Like I told you the other day, my boys are always looking for a mom. I try to think of ways to put them around women, short of getting married, of course."

He smiled as he said this, but she wondered if she blushed. What he'd said about marriage hit too close to home for her to find the words genuinely amusing. Did he ever think of remarrying? She was curious about his late wife and their relationship. Had they had a good marriage? Did he miss her and compare everyone he met to her? She wasn't going to come right out and ask him, but she couldn't help wanting to know.

"How long has she been gone?" she asked, hoping this would open up the subject and answer some of her questions.

He looked at her as if surprised by the question and hesitated. "Three years," he said.

She waited for him to say more, but it seemed that his wife and her passing were a closed subject.

There was a long silence, and then Fitz reached over and briefly touched her hand. "I need to tell you about the people David is involved with."

"What do you mean?"

"We've been watching these guys for some time," he said. "They're not amateurs."

"If you knew David—" she started to protest, but he interrupted.

"David is just one player, and a minor one. The people he's connected with are ruthless. You *must* take them seriously. Although we've got your children hidden away, I would like to see you off this case. Even if you're on their side, you don't want to have anything to do with them."

She wanted to protest, but knew he was right.

Now, waiting for Fitz to exit the elevator, she wondered

how he had known to find her at the office. It was Saturday, so officially the law firm was closed, and no one was in but her. She looked down at what she had on and regretted her decision to wear a sheer, flowing sundress. It was comfortable and cool, particularly when the air conditioning punked out, which it had earlier, but it was almost like a nightgown and not very professional. Although they'd shared kisses in North Carolina, nothing had gone on between them since, and she was suddenly feeling bashful.

But there was no time to worry about that now. She heard the elevator come to a shuddering halt, signaling Fitz's arrival.

Quickly she reached under her desk in search of her sandals, which she'd discarded while she worked. They were nowhere to be found, and when she heard a sharp rap at the door, she gave up and went, in her bare feet, to answer it.

"Mary Ellen," she heard him shout as she approached the door. "Open up. It's me."

Fitz hadn't been able to get her out of his mind since he had left her the day before. She had been such a trouper about leaving her children. When he watched her with them at the airport, he thought he was going to lose it himself. It was clear that they were everything to her, but even so, she would rather give them up than risk their lives. She probably had to stay on this case, but she was one of the good guys. He'd bet his career that she was. And maybe that's exactly what he was doing, because he had just successfully convinced his people that she was trustworthy. But he wasn't so sure he was happy about the outcome of that encounter. In fact, he wondered if she and he had been better off when he still didn't trust her. He didn't want her to get hurt, and if she was involved, that was always a risk. But the card had been played and he couldn't take it back. He had to be much more careful about how he played the rest of his hand.

Which meant that he had to concentrate, no matter how sexy she looked. For there she was, standing at the open door in some sort of flimsy Indian-print dress. He had all he could do to keep himself from staring. What he hadn't been prepared for was how the sight of her bare toes peeking out from under the gossamer fabric turned all of his senses up to high voltage. Which explained why it was several moments before he realized that she was asking him a question.

"Are the children really okay?" she asked. "You aren't just saying that to make me feel better?"

For a minute he looked at her as if she were speaking in tongues, then he shook his head and focused on her in typical coplike fashion. "John, the one who saw them this morning, was very clear. He says they seem to be adjusting well and that the house where they are staying has a built-in pool. They seemed to like that," he said, attempting a smile in the face of her obvious grief. "I know this is difficult. We'll try to figure out a way for you to communicate with them."

She nodded with relief. For the first time, she was sure she had done the right thing in sending them away. Of course she knew they couldn't stay here, but until now she hadn't been sure if a stranger's house was any better.

Now that she knew the children were okay, she noticed him. He looked wonderful dressed in khakis and blue dress shirt, a neatly folded tie sticking out of his breast pocket, and his blazer over his shoulder. Mary Ellen tried to hide her appreciation. She wished she had a sweater to cover her bareness, or that she had at least found her misplaced sandals. Self-consciously, she folded her arms across her chest.

But it was only an instant before his eyes met hers. "Can we talk in your office? There are some important things we need to discuss—not about the children."

Puzzled, she shrugged and motioned for him to follow her

back to her office, turning in that direction so Fitz wouldn't see how flustered she was. She tried to compose herself as she walked down the hall ahead of him. But for that one long look, he'd barely glanced at her except to stare intensely into her eyes, as if on a mission. What was going on?

She felt more secure when she was safely seated behind her desk. At least she had stacks of papers and piles of books to hide behind.

"Sorry to intrude like this," he began, then paused, perhaps to collect his thoughts or to let her know that what he was about to say was important. He didn't look happy.

"What's up?" she asked.

He sighed in resignation. "I've got a proposal for you, from the top. They want you to stay with the case. Stay on as David's attorney."

She sat back, so startled she forgot to cover her chest. "Are you serious?"

"I'm afraid so."

"But you said this case is dangerous."

"It is. And I don't want you to do it. It's the FBI that does. They think you're the only one who can help us break through."

"What do you mean?"

"Remember how I told you that we knew who David was working for?"

"Uh-huh."

"Well, we know who he works directly for, and we know their contact in Europe. What we don't know is who their head man is in the United States. What the people I work for, the Feds, are hoping, is that at some point the head guy will contact you. Then you will be able to lead us to him."

"Do you think that's possible?"

He shrugged. "Probably. But I don't want you to do it. It's very dangerous."

"But are you saying it's the only way to get to him?" She leaned forward, as if afraid to miss a word, intensely aware of the implications of what she was being asked to do.

"Yeah, but that doesn't mean you have to be the one."

"I'm not sure I can get out of this case, anyway. David's father won't agree, so David probably won't either. That means I'll have to make a very compelling argument to the judge, which will likely cause some ugly publicity for the Andersons, which my boss won't like." She shrugged. "And there's no guarantee that the judge will agree to let me out, no matter how compelling the argument." She didn't say anything for a minute, lost in thought. "What if I just keep my eyes open and stay in? I'll be careful." She'd suddenly realized she wanted to do it. She wanted to help put this monster away. He'd threatened her children. He deserved whatever they could give him.

"That's what the Feds say. They're not looking for a martyr. But I don't want you to do it at all."

"Maybe I don't have a choice."

He scowled and shook his head. "Don't think like that. Of course you have a choice. You get out of this case. You get your children back. You get on with your life."

"If only it were that easy. I'd give anything to be with my children. But from what you're telling me, this thing isn't going to be over until they get these guys. Why would they suddenly leave me alone if I stopped representing David? Since I'm stuck, I might as well be some help."

She looked over at him, hoping he'd convince her otherwise. Instead he just nodded somberly.

"So I'm right?" she whispered. "I really am stuck in the middle until it's over?"

"I'm afraid so. I don't want you to be, but I think you are. Somehow you got picked."

"The phone calls," she said.

He nodded. "For starters. Obviously they've been watching

you. They must have decided you were a good person to use. They might even have tapped your phone. We're checking on that."

"So who is David working for? Someone who knows me?"

Fitz shook his head. "The Feds don't want you to know. They think you'll be better off if you remain in the dark. You won't slip if you don't know anything. Are you okay with that?"

"I guess. It doesn't sound as if I have much choice." She shuddered, wondering who David was working for and if they watched her all the time.

Perhaps he'd read her mind, because his next words responded to her fears. "I've asked to be assigned to you to protect you. They've agreed, but we have to be careful. We can't let them know we're suspicious. But that's my problem, not yours. All you need to know is that I'll be doing my best to protect you."

Well, that was some comfort. Maybe the only comfort she had right now.

The front office door rattled. Someone was trying to get in. Mary Ellen looked at Fitz in alarm. Were the people who were threatening her bold enough to come right to her office? If so, she was ready to hide and let him do the shooting.

He motioned her to slide down under her desk. She did as he asked, at the same time watching him take his gun out. He flattened himself against the wall next to the office door and cautiously peered out.

Chapter Fifteen

Anyone here?" came a familiar voice.

She slowly peeked out from under the desk and met the eyes of Mr. Boylan, the firm's other senior partner. He was the last person Mary Ellen expected to see in the office on a beautiful summer Saturday afternoon.

"Just me," she squeaked, hoisting herself out from under the desk and back into her chair. At the same time, Fitz hastily stuffed his gun back into its case and came forward to greet the man.

Boylan was not someone she wanted to run into right now. She wasn't anxious to explain why she was hiding under her desk, casually dressed, in the company of a hot guy. Boylan was the office's biggest gossip.

But instead of commenting, all he asked was why she wasn't on vacation as planned. Before explaining, Mary Ellen introduced Fitz and endured Boylan's speculative appraisal as she tried in vain to come up with a reasonable-sounding excuse as to why she was not at the shore.

Mr. Boylan didn't wait for an explanation. "That means you'll be able to come to our party tonight," he said, including Fitz in his command.

She nodded dumbly, too surprised to come up with a plausible excuse. But from Boylan's tone, no was probably not an option. Besides, the event was important for her job and she should go, no matter what else was going on in her life.

Mary Ellen thought longingly of the shore as they parked and approached the Boylans' house. Even from the street they could hear the music as she and Fitz followed the path around the house. The Boylans' backyard, with its glowing lanterns, was the perfect setting for a party. It looked as if, at half past eight, most of the guests had arrived. Small groups of people deep in conversation filled the patio and the tables surrounding it.

They were serving wine, beer, and margaritas at the bar, and trays of canapés were being passed around. Fitz took her order for wine and headed for the bar. She waited for him in the middle of the yard filled with her colleagues and wondered how she was going to cope. She couldn't let on to anyone that her children were being threatened. She also was not about to admit that Fitz was not her date, but a bodyguard.

He wasn't acting much like a bodyguard. When he returned with her wine, his appreciative survey of her appearance made her feel suddenly shy. At the same time, she was glad that she had decided on a brightly colored sundress, which made her feel confident and sexy. But Fitz's appreciation reminded her of the complicated relationship they now had. Fleeting thoughts of Kevin Costner and Whitney Houston in *The Bodyguard* didn't help in the slightest.

It also didn't help that Fitz looked great himself, in pressed khakis and a starched blue and white striped shirt that showed off his tan. She forced such thoughts out of her mind as she noticed Michael Stein, whom she worked closely with, heading toward her with his wife.

"I didn't expect to see you here," he said after she introduced him and his wife to Fitz. "Aren't you supposed to be down at the shore?"

She nodded, ready to deliver the excuse Fitz and she had come up with earlier. "I got a call from a neighbor, the one watching the cats, about a leaking pipe. I figured I better come up and check it out before there was real damage. Now that I'm back, I decided to stay and take time off later."

Michael nodded sympathetically. "The kids must have been disappointed."

Feeling guilty for her lies, even if they were necessary, Mary Ellen shook her head. "I got someone to keep an eye on them so they didn't have to come back. They haven't been away all summer and were looking forward to the time at the beach so much, I didn't have the heart."

Before she had to explain any further, the music got faster and louder and several people started to dance. She turned to Fitz, who nodded as he took her hand and led her into the center of the crowd.

Their escape was brief. Her early return and her escort prompted curiosity. When the music stopped, two more associates approached, and she noticed that a third cornered Fitz. Marilyn—dubbed Betty Boop by her office mates—acknowledged Mary Ellen after a few minutes. "Your friend was just telling me that he's a cop. How dangerous!" she gushed.

Mary Ellen just smiled and nodded, intending to let her continue to fawn over Fitz, until she noticed Marilyn leaning toward him and brushing her hand against his leg as she did so.

"Excuse us, will you?" she smiled at Marilyn, before taking Fitz firmly by the hand. "There are several people I want to introduce him to."

When she glanced sideways at him she caught a look of amusement.

"What are you laughing at?" she growled, trying not to feel foolish.

"Were you jealous?"

"Of course not. I was just trying to save you."

To her annoyance, instead of responding, he just continued to laugh softly. But her irritation subsided when he slipped his arm around her and pulled her closer. He leaned down and whispered in her ear, "You don't really think I was interested, do you? By now you should know me better than that."

She tried not to think about what that implied. She needed to get through so much before she could concentrate on what might be going on between them. It thrilled her all the same.

While she and Fitz talked to first one and then another of the partners and associates in her office, he kept his arm possessively around her waist. It crossed her mind to brush off his hand. She wasn't sure if she wanted people in her office to see such a display. But she didn't brush it off.

She might have allowed herself to believe that they were, in fact, a couple if it weren't for the arrival of the Susinos. John and his wife, as well as several of the other U.S. Attorneys whom the firm dealt with regularly, had been invited. The look on John's face when he saw Fitz brought her back to reality. It was clear John knew why Fitz was there and probably also why Mary Ellen was at the party instead of down at the shore.

Still, she could have ignored all that if it weren't for John and Fitz going off into a corner together and seriously conferring for the next half hour. Observing them, Rose, John's wife, looked at Mary Ellen and whispered, "I don't know whether to ask what's going on between you and Fitz or between Fitz and John. Obviously they are into something serious. Is that why Fitz is here?"

Mary Ellen just shook her head and tried to keep a smile on

her face. Rose must have realized there was no point in pursuing it and changed the subject by asking about her kids. Again Mary Ellen was in a dilemma. But her experience as a mother paid off. Instead of answering Rose's question about the twins, Mary Ellen asked about Rose's oldest son, who was on the soccer team with Tim. Jack Susino had an amazing knack for getting into trouble, and Rose usually had a story about his latest mishap. Tonight was no exception. Fifteen minutes later, when Fitz and John rejoined them, Rose was still on the subject of Jack and his latest escapade. John just grinned when he realized what they were talking about, but Fitz looked distracted and soon made excuses for them to circulate.

"Sorry to go off with John like that," he whispered to her when he had her alone. "There have been some developments in the case."

She looked at him to say more. He shook his head. "The less you know, the better."

She nodded in frustration. "It's nothing to do with the children, is it?"

He briefly pulled her to him and pressed his lips to her forehead. "Of course not," he said softly. "Your children are fine. If there was anything new with them, I would tell you." He let go of her and looked around at the partying crowd. "We better join this group before anyone gets suspicious, or starts commenting about your new boyfriend's lack of manners."

She grinned as he led her back into the center of the crowd. For tonight, she resolved, she would stop fighting the inevitable and enjoy being with him. When it came time to sit down to dinner—at the several cloth-covered round tables set out around the patio—Fitz made sure there was a place for the two of them with John and Rose Susino.

At dinner when John started to reminisce about law school, bringing up ancient stories from their first year, she looked over to Fitz. She wasn't sure how he would react.

"How long ago was this?" asked Fitz, clearly interested.

"Had to be fourteen years ago. Right?" said John, looking up at Mary Ellen and Rose for confirmation. They both nodded.

"You went to law school right out of college?" Fitz asked Mary Ellen.

"Just about. I worked for a year as a paralegal first, and saved some money before I went."

"So what was she like fourteen years ago?" Fitz asked John. "All buttoned up, prim and proper?"

John laughed and shook his head. "Crusader is more like it." He smiled, remembering. "The first time I met her, she was at a Lawyers Guild meeting, looking all serious in her wire-rimmed glasses and her straight hair down to her waist, leading a discussion on prisoners' rights. She was so determined to save the world that I was intimidated, until I realized she was wearing a Mickey Mouse wristwatch. No one who wears a watch like that could be that serious."

Fitz looked surprised. "Is that true?"

Mary Ellen nodded with chagrin. "I was just like every other law student then. We were all ultra serious and concerned about everyone's constitutional rights. Remember?"

Several people at the table nodded, for which Mary Ellen was grateful. One woman even began a story of her own student days—about her first rally at an Earth Day demonstration. When she concluded, Mary Ellen explained, "It was the time. We were all involved. We thought we could make a difference."

This time when she looked around the table for confirmation, she caught Fitz's eye. When he smiled at her, it was as if a bolt of lightning shot right through her, bringing her up short. Although nothing was said, in that one exchange of glances, it was clear that there was something between them that needed to be addressed. For the rest of the party, he was never out of her thoughts and she was always aware of his presence. She knew he was thinking of her too. He never took his eyes off her, and more significantly, if his hand wasn't on her shoulder or arm, then his leg was pressed against hers. She could hardly think about anything but him.

By the time dinner was over and Fitz was driving Mary Ellen home, the questions she had about Fitz had percolated to the surface and she had resolved that she couldn't get involved with him, not until the case was closed. She needed to keep her distance before she made a fool of herself and lived to regret it.

When they pulled into her driveway, Fitz put the car in park and turned to Mary Ellen as she reached for the door. "What's wrong? Are you okay?"

"I'm fine. Really."

He shook his head. "You're obviously upset about something. Won't you tell me what's going on?"

"I can't," she said, opening the door and sliding out. "It's too difficult to explain. I have to go in."

She bolted out of the car and rushed up the path to her doorway, afraid to turn around in case she weakened.

But no sooner did she reach the door and put her key in the lock than he was right behind her. "Mary Ellen," he said, putting his hand on her shoulder. "Don't leave it like this. No matter what you think, I've got to look out for you."

She slowly looked up, wishing the streetlight were brighter so she could read the expression on his face.

"Tell me what's wrong. Did something happen back there at the party that I missed? The whole ride back, you were so quiet, and then you bolted out of the car. You even left your bag," he said, holding up her purse.

She shook her head as she took it from him. "Sorry. I didn't mean to be rude. There's nothing wrong. Nothing happened. I just need to be alone."

"I see."

"No. You probably don't."

He shook his head. "I know I've been giving you mixed signals. Spending all that time with John at the party, but not telling you what's going on. I don't blame you for bolting. Smart thing to do. Smarter than what I'm doing, or trying to do," he continued, letting his voice trail off as he stood there looking at her in the moonlight.

Now that her eyes had adjusted to the dark, she could see him more clearly. His eyes met hers. Without a word, not conscious of having made a decision, she walked into his open arms, and he gathered her up and held on to her as if his life depended on it.

"What am I going to do about you?" he whispered. "You can't sneak away from me. I'm supposed to be watching out for you."

"I was afraid," she explained, her face pressed against his chest.

"I know. I am too. But I can't keep away from you."

She nodded. "It's crazy. And it's going to make things harder and more complicated," she said, pushing him away to see him better and look into his eyes.

He nodded. "Don't I know it. I shouldn't even be here, this visible. I'm leaving—just as soon as you are safely inside."

She nodded, understanding that was what they must do.

Chapter Sixteen

It was all Fitz could do to stand there and let her go into the house alone. She'd looked so beautiful at the party, he was sure he wasn't the only man who wanted to take her home. In spite of how her heart was breaking, and he knew it was, she talked about nothing but her children during the ride over. She still managed to go to the party ready to have fun, clothed in a bright, silky dress that, without being obvious, called attention to her long slim curves, highlighting each attribute. But there was something more: an extra sparkle in her eye and a subtle note to her voice that pushed him nearly over the edge. It was all he could do not to drag her away from her colleagues so he could be alone with her and follow his instincts. And now he stood here as she entered her house, alone.

Steeling himself against the temptation to do otherwise, he thrust his hands in his pockets and stolidly stood by his car at the edge of her driveway. He waited for her to give the signal, the blinking of the front hall light, before he headed home.

When the light didn't blink immediately, he was on guard, ready to dash onto the front porch and break down her front door. Then he heard a crash from inside, and he was at her door in an instant, gun drawn. Suddenly another light, further inside the house, went on and then, just as he was about to find a way through the locked door, the front door opened. "Are you okay? Is everything all right?"

"I think maybe someone's been here," she said, her voice shaky. She seemed close to tears.

His mouth went dry and he could feel his body go into attack mode, but he forced back his anger and fear. "Why do you think that?" he said, striding in and giving the room the once-over. When he saw nothing immediate to alarm him, he pulled her trembling body into his arms.

She stayed there, not saying a word, as he held her tight and ran his hand down her back, trying to reassure her. She took several deep breaths and then gently pulled free. When she spoke, her voice was under control. "I don't want to be overdramatic, but the front light was out, which doesn't make sense. I just replaced the bulb." They looked up above them. The socket was empty. "That's not all," she said, barely managing to get the words out. "In the living room, one of the chairs was in the middle of the room. That's what I tripped over when I went in to turn on the light. Someone has obviously moved it." She paused and looked around the hallway and living room. "Maybe they used it to stand on when they removed the bulb."

Fitz nodded. "Let's get you out of here. We don't want to take any chances. I'm going to call for backup. We'll search the place."

She nodded somberly.

Two local squad cars appeared in minutes. It was another ten before the men from his unit in Newark arrived. With all of them working, they were able to quickly go through the house to determine that nothing else was amiss while Mary Ellen waited impatiently in his car. Fitz came out to tell her everything was secure.

"I want to go back in and look around for myself," she said. "Maybe I was wrong. Maybe there is another explanation."

"Does someone else have a set of keys to your house?"

She nodded. "Sure. The neighbor across the street and Heidi."

"Could one of them have come in and moved things around like that?"

"Mr. Taylor would have no reason to go in. He only has the key in case one of the children loses theirs. He was petsitting for us while we were away, but the cats stayed over at his house." She paused as if thinking. "I suppose Heidi might have come in. I can't imagine why, but she does have the run of the place."

"Give them both a call now and see if either of them might have been here."

She nodded reluctantly. "I hate to wake Mr. Taylor."

Fitz grinned. "Somehow, after all the turmoil and police activity over here, I doubt he's asleep. In fact, he'll probably be glad to find out what's going on."

Fitz had been right. Mr. Taylor was awake and happy to get the scoop on why the police were there. But he hadn't been in her house, nor had he seen anyone hanging around the property.

There was no answer at Heidi's. While she was on the phone, though, she noticed that she had a voice mail on her cell phone.

It was from Kirk Anderson. "My people are looking into your problem," he said, "so I wouldn't worry too much. As for David's court date, he'll meet with you on Monday down at the courthouse, an hour before you're scheduled to appear. That should give you plenty of time."

His message almost made her forget about her latest crisis. Whatever else was going on, she still had to represent David. She was also irritated by Anderson's high-handed manner. An hour wasn't enough time to prepare David, but from the tone of the call, the time and place of the meeting was an order, not a suggestion. Under any other circumstances, she wouldn't put up with his imperious attitude, but with her children's safety at risk and the source of the threats still unknown, she wasn't about to confront him. She hoped Kirk Anderson would at least let her talk to his son alone.

She saved the message and went into the kitchen to find something for them to drink. Fitz wanted her to leave the house and spend the night at the Susinos', but she was determined to stay where she was. It was bad enough that she'd had to hide her children; they weren't going to make her flee too. Besides, maybe she'd been wrong about there being an intruder. Maybe Heidi had been here, or maybe she had been so distracted that she had left that chair like that. She was so tired and confused, she didn't know what to think.

But it was nice to sit on the front porch with Fitz after the commotion had died down.

"So that's Anderson," said Fitz. She had replayed the message for him. "Sounds like a general giving orders. All your clients like that?"

"Nope. Just him."

"Kind of strange, isn't it, that he doesn't want you to see David until just before the court hearing?"

She nodded. "Very strange, but typical. He's a control freak," she explained. "None of us have free access to his files, only Dunphy. I just hope he isn't going to stay when I talk to David. And if he brings his wife, I'm really out of luck. She'll just carry on about how poor David couldn't have done it—whatever *it* might be."

Fitz was quiet for a minute, and then turned to her. "How much do you know about Anderson, anyway?"

Mary Ellen was surprised by the question. Kirk Anderson? In the office everyone dealt with him with kid gloves because that's the way Dunphy wanted it, and Dunphy was the senior partner. She'd gone along with treating him that way, since she rarely had anything to do with him, except when David was in trouble. Most of her work was civil litigation, usually breach of contracts or personal injury cases for other clients. Now that she tried to explain what Kirk Anderson did, she realized that outside of a few of his cases and her involvement with David, she knew very little about him. "He's an old friend of Mr. Dunphy's," she said. "I think they went to high school together. And he runs a company that has enough business to keep Dunphy happily on golf courses the world over."

"What kind of business is it?"

"Export/import."

"Really? That's interesting." The way he scrunched his eyebrows together as if in serious thought made her think that maybe Fitz found the subject of Anderson's business more than just interesting.

"What exactly does Anderson export?"

She had to think for a minute; she knew so little about what he did. "All kinds of things," she said, trying to remember specifics, "primarily from Eastern Europe," she added. Then when he looked puzzled, she searched her brain and pulled out information she had forgotten she knew. "I think Anderson started the company, back in the seventies, by importing pottery from one of his wife's cousin's towns in Poland. From what I understand, although I have no direct knowledge, he keeps adding other products whenever he sees an opportunity."

She tried to remember if she knew anything else, at the same time determining if what she was telling Fitz was a matter of public record and not privileged. "I don't know much more than that," she said. "According to Mr. Dunphy, the secret to Anderson's success is that if he has a shipment of goods coming into the United States from Eastern Europe, then that same container will go back to Europe loaded with something of ours. That way there's no waste."

"Economical."

"Yeah, on a grand scale. I gather he's made a lot of money from it."

Fitz looked at his watch, put his glass down, and rose to his feet. "So what do you say? Are you going to be sensible and go to the Susinos'?"

She shook her head. "I can't let these people intimidate me. This is my home. Besides, who is going to look after my cats?"

He shrugged. "What if you ask Mr. Taylor to keep looking after the cats, and we find a hotel room for you?"

When she shook her head firmly, he stopped arguing and moved on to plan B. "The local precinct has promised me that they will keep an eye on you. They should be patrolling the house, driving by all through the day and night. If there's anything odd or unusual, call them right away. Okay?"

Then, after making sure every window in the house was bolted shut and securing Mary Ellen's promise that she would set the alarm as soon as he left, Fitz got ready to head home.

As she walked him to the door, she only half listened to him tell her to be conscientious about setting the alarm. She was wondering if he would kiss her good night, or if, because he was in work mode, he would be all business. She almost wished he would skip the kiss. Based on past experience, she knew a kiss would only leave her frustrated and wanting.

Perhaps because she was so preoccupied, she was thoroughly taken by surprise when Fitz suddenly pulled her toward him, into the shelter of his arms, and pressed his lips against hers. She didn't need to be reminded of how his touch stirred up deep feelings and desires. But it still came as a shock when their lips met and his touch ignited the powerful emotions that his near presence always set off. When he pulled her closer and kissed her harder, she hungrily responded. He pulled her even closer and ran a trail of kisses from her mouth down her neck and collarbone. It felt so good to be in his arms.

Suddenly, he let her go. "This is crazy," he said, his voice husky with desire. "I've got to get out of here, before I am unable to."

He was right, of course. "I know," she said when she managed to find her voice. "I usually am not so—" she tried to explain.

Before she could say more, he reached over and ran his finger over her lips. "I want you to be like this. I wish I could stay," he said softly. "I want to be with you when you're not under pressure, aren't worrying about your children, and aren't being totally sensible. All through the party I kept thinking how much I wanted to bring you back here, take you in my arms, and not worry about anything but being with you." He pulled her closer, gently this time. As he held her and stroked her back, he continued. "When all of this is over, we'll make time to be alone together."

She watched him go, forcing herself to continue to smile as she shut the door. But after he was gone, she felt more lost and alone than she had ever felt, even in the worst days at the end of her marriage. It wasn't that she was afraid. Knowing there would be a squad car passing by made her believe that, at least for tonight, she was safe. What upset her was how much she wanted to be with Fitz. Now that he was in her life, she wanted him with her all the time. Shaking her head at her foolishness, she marched upstairs and tucked herself into bed, where she tried to lose herself in the late-night movie.

The phone rang a short while later. "Hi, it's me," Fitz said. "I wanted to hear your voice and know you were okay."

She understood. She felt the same way. "I know—"

"When all of this is over . . . ," he interrupted.

She nodded, unable to respond, frustration and longing overwhelming her. She almost wished he hadn't called. Hearing his voice and knowing he couldn't be with her made the pain more real.

The rest of the weekend was even worse. She missed her children terribly and couldn't stand walking past their empty bedrooms. It didn't help when she got a phone call on Sunday night from her ex-husband, Chris.

"What's happening up there?" he sputtered into the phone.

"Chris?" she said, quickly recognizing his voice and his abrupt way. "What is it? What do you want?"

"I'm the one looking for answers," he barked. "Why am I getting calls about the kids?"

Her chest tightened instantly. She should have told him what was going on. It hadn't even crossed her mind, she'd been so concerned about the children and their safety. "What do you mean? Who's been calling? What did they say?"

"I don't know who they are. They refused to identify themselves, so I didn't answer their questions, but they wanted to know if the kids were with me. What's this about? Are you in some kind of trouble? Are the kids in danger?"

She breathed deeply, trying to calm herself enough to deal with her ex-husband. He would not be happy with her answers. "I started getting phone calls last week," she began, explaining about the threats and what she had done about it. She skipped the part about Fitz or their stay in North Carolina, but did tell him that the FBI was involved.

"You should have called me when you started getting the calls!"

"I know," she admitted, "my mistake."

"They could have come down and stayed with me."

"But that's the point," she explained, relieved that he wasn't too angry with her about not telling him. "They would have found them at your house. If they're calling you, it's obvious that they don't know where the children are."

He conceded that she was right, and perhaps because he too was worried about their children and for the first time in many years they were on the same side, he was unexpectedly civil. He made her promise to keep him informed and then as the conversation was ending, interrupted their good-byes. "The kids tell you about the baby?" he asked.

"As a matter of fact, they did," she said, surprised he brought it up.

"They okay with it?"

His concern was uncharacteristic. Perhaps he was developing a new sensitivity as he approached middle age. Theirs had not been a happy union. Work had been his first priority almost from the time they were first married. Even so, it had come as a surprise when he told her that he was leaving her for his secretary. Since he also was moving out of state for a new job, too far to see the kids on a regular basis, she questioned his love for them. But he did sound concerned tonight. It could be that he genuinely cared for their children and had just never known how to show it.

"I think so," she replied, trying to be fair with him since he seemed to be making an effort himself. "Just try to include them as much as you can. If you do, I think they will be fine with it."

"Yeah," he said softly. "I'll do that. Thanks."

She hung up the phone and, with lingering thoughts of their conversation, went downstairs to lock up for the night. She would be dealing with the Andersons tomorrow and needed plenty of sleep so she could cope. Unfortunately, that didn't seem to be in the cards because when she called to her cats to come in, although the older two instantly responded—they always did when food was involved—the baby did not. For the next hour she called Minky's name and finally, when the cat still did not come in, she dressed and went out in search of him despite the rain. When midnight approached and the kitten still had not shown up, she reluctantly gave up the search, reassuring herself that it was a mild summer night and that the cat would find shelter.

* * *

Morning finally came and she pushed aside her worries about the children, the phone call from Chris, and the missing kitten. She needed to concentrate on what was ahead, dealing with David and his intrusive and controlling father. As she left the house, she noticed a manila envelope propped against the front door.

Nothing prepared her for what she found inside the envelope: a photograph of her kitten, Minky, obviously dead. Horrified, she dropped the photo. Even without looking closely, she could tell what had happened. Her hands shook as she reached down and picked up the photo, trying to keep a rein on her panic and sorrow.

Her children would be devastated. She should never have let the cats out the night before. She should have kept looking until she found Minky. As her two cats circled around her and rubbed against her legs, she thought about what she would tell her children. Who would do such a cruel and senseless thing to an innocent animal? And where were Fitz's men? Weren't they supposed to be watching the house? Might they know who was responsible?

Just after she arrived at her office, she got a call from the same man who'd been threatening her.

"Let that be a lesson to you," he said when she picked up. "Now you know that we are always watching you. If you have anything more to do with Fitzpatrick, we will do the same to your children."

Chapter Seventeen

Mary Ellen couldn't let Minky's death or her children's absence distract her from her job. She'd never get David off, get her children back, find out who killed Minky, and learn who was behind all this terror if she did.

So in spite of all that had happened, Mary Ellen was waiting outside the courtroom at the appointed hour. David was not there. When Kirk and Lois Anderson arrived ten minutes later, David wasn't with them. "He's parking the car," his father explained. "I wanted to talk to you first.

"Lois," he said, turning to his wife. "You go wait in the courtroom. I need to talk to Mary Ellen alone."

Lois Anderson nodded and lowered her eyes, not meeting Mary Ellen's gaze. Mary Ellen had met her on several other occasions and it was always the same. Although she was an attractive, well-dressed matron who looked as if she could take on anyone, when her husband spoke, Lois did what she was told. The only time she behaved otherwise was when she thought her husband or Mary Ellen were expecting too much of David. It had happened the last time David went to court.

Lois Anderson thought the owner of the tavern should drop the charges, under the theory that "boys will be boys." Mary Ellen knew that was not realistic, and Kirk Anderson himself seemed to feel that it would be wrong for David to go unpunished. Mary Ellen wondered what Lois Anderson's take would be on the charges that David was now facing.

Kirk Anderson waited until they were alone in the hall. "We're counting on you," he said after closing the door.

She nodded. He had already made that quite clear.

"You understand that." He looked her square in the eye and wagged his finger at her. "I won't have him serving time for some trumped-up charge. It would break his mother's heart. She believes he had nothing to do with it."

He was so different from the cool power broker she was used to seeing that she almost felt sorry for him. The man did seem to care about his wife and son.

"I'm going to do my best," she said. "But don't you think there might be something to the charges? David certainly wasn't the mastermind behind any car-theft ring, but isn't it possible that he might have been involved?"

He shrugged. "Who knows? But you gotta fix it. Get him off. I don't want her upset."

She tried to ignore his indifference to justice or the truth. Even if she could rationalize his attitude by saying he was just trying to protect his wife, she couldn't ignore that he had probably transmitted this attitude to his son. "I'll do what I can. But first I've got to talk to David."

David finally showed up, minutes later. His father gave him a long, hard look before turning to Mary Ellen. "You wanted to see David alone? Here he is. I'll be in the courtroom with the missus. Call me if you need anything. Otherwise, you got about ten minutes before court time."

"I got lost," David explained. "I was wandering around the other end of the building. If they didn't make these places so confusing, all the halls and doors going every which way, I might have gotten here on time. As it is, it's lucky I'm here at all."

She shook her head and stared at him, observing that he was his usual disheveled self, his clothes wrinkled, his hair uncombed, his face obviously in need of a shave. But more than his appearance, it was his manner that worried Mary Ellen. He had such an air of defensiveness and a way of acting guilty before anyone even accused him of anything, it was unlikely he would make a good impression on the judge.

He was also strangely agitated. "What's she doin' here?" he suddenly muttered.

Mary Ellen looked around but saw no one except a young blond woman talking to several men in suits.

Mary Ellen took David by the elbow and quickly walked him to the small conference room a short way down the hall, where they would have more privacy.

"Who is that woman? What are you talking about? You're not making any sense." She shook her head with frustration. "With you being late, we have hardly any time to discuss your response to these allegations. Don't go off on some tangent and waste the little time we do have."

David shrugged his shoulders and did not answer her.

She eyed him with concern and wondered how best to communicate with him. He could be unpredictable, and anything could set him off. She wondered if it stemmed from his father's controlling personality, or if there was something about his mother's ineffectiveness that had resulted in his inability to take responsibility for himself.

"I've been set up!" David said, suddenly erupting. "What's it called? Entrapped? Yeah! I've been entrapped!"

"By whom? That woman? If that's the case, you need to tell me about it."

He looked startled, as if remembering that up until now he'd claimed total ignorance.

"I didn't do it. What she says is a lie."

She almost felt sorry for him. "David, I'm your attorney, not your mother. I'm not here to judge you. I just want to know what's going on so I can be prepared to respond. If there is some woman who's going to testify against you, you need to tell me about her so I can deal with it."

David nodded, though he didn't look convinced.

"You've been saying you're innocent—that you had nothing to do with the car thefts," Mary Ellen continued. "Are you now telling me there's a woman that could be a witness against you? What's the real story?"

His eyes darted nervously around the small room, as if afraid someone might be able to overhear. "The blond in the hall talking to some guys. I know her. From the bar I hang out in."

"The one that you trashed."

"Yeah," he said, making a feeble attempt to hide a smirk. "That's the place. Anyway, I used to see her there. Buy her a drink sometimes. Dance with her and talk to her and her friend. She was always real friendly. Now I know why. And it explains," he added, almost to himself, "why she hasn't been around. I kind of wondered."

"And you what—stole a car for her?" Mary Ellen asked, trying to get him back on track.

"Sort of. She said she knew someone who was looking for hard-to-find parts. She wanted to know if I could help her out."

"And could you?"

"Sure. Lots of people can. Believe me. If you needed parts for your car . . . do you?"

She shook her head. The guy was incorrigible.

"Well, if you did, you could get some. Probably by calling and asking me or somebody like me."

"You mean someone who deals in stolen cars."

"Well, I wouldn't put it like that. I mean someone who has *contacts*. She knew from the bar that I knew people."

"So you spoke to someone."

"I might of. As I said, I know a lot of people."

"And these people you know. What did they do for her? Get her parts?"

"Did I say that? Never. What do you take me for, a criminal?"

"David! You can't have it both ways. Either you didn't do it and you never saw her before in your life, or you did, but were set up. Which way do you want it?" She paused and tried to think of the most effective way to make him understand that he had to tell her the truth—that it was for his own good. "You've got to stop fudging on this and tell me what's really going on. As it is, we're totally unprepared for today because you wouldn't meet with me. They've obviously got hard evidence. Are you or are you not involved in a car theft ring?"

He looked around uneasily, as if afraid someone would hear him.

"Does my mother have to know?" he whispered.

"Probably." Even she lowered her voice and looked around, as if afraid Lois Anderson might hear. But why David would care more about his mother knowing than his dad was beyond her. "More to the point, as your attorney, you've got to tell me. And if we're going to defend these allegations by saying you were entrapped, you'll have to admit you did it."

At that moment, before David had a chance to respond, Kirk Anderson charged into the small conference room.

"They look like they're ready to begin. You better get in there," he ordered breathlessly. Perspiration was dripping from his face. Was Anderson all right? It would be a fine mess to have a major client keel over in the courtroom as a result of anxiety about the way an associate was handling his son's case.

Suddenly Anderson seemed to pull himself together, focusing on her as he spoke. "The judge just walked into the courtroom."

"We'll be right there," she said. "I need one more minute."

"Everything okay, son?" he asked, turning to David. "You've told Mrs. Carey that you were with us on the night they're talking about?"

"Not yet, Dad," said David, looking uneasy. "I haven't had a chance."

"Well, take care of it, son. You don't have all day. The judge is looking for you."

With a quick glance back at Mary Ellen, he charged out of the room after saying he'd tell the judge they'd be right there.

"What was that all about?"

"I was with my parents. Like he said," David mumbled, refusing to meet her eyes.

"David! If that's the case, why is this the first I'm hearing of it? What about that woman? How does she fit into all this?"

"I just know her. Like I said, from the bar."

She shook her head. Of course he was lying, and obviously at the direction of his father. What could she do about it?

Make David tell her the whole story. That was her only choice. "David," she said, trying to hide her irritation and frustration, "remember, you will be under oath when you testify."

He nodded, still not looking at her. "What if she asked me to? Does that mean they can't get me?"

"It might. That's what we're here to find out," she said. "But we won't know unless you explain what happened."

He just shook his head.

"Well, we've got to get in there," she said. "There's no more time to talk about it now. Just remember, once you're sworn in, anything you say is under oath. If you lie, you're committing perjury, and if they can prove it, you can do time for that too."

"I know," he said. "I'm not going to lie."

She wished she could believe him, but she knew he was weak and could be talked into almost anything.

Chapter Eighteen

They walked into the courtroom just as their case was called. Mary Ellen told David to take a seat at the counsel table. His parents were already sitting right behind them in the first row. She set her files on the table and looked toward the front of the courtroom.

"Good morning, Your Honor," she greeted Judge Morris, eyeing him curiously. He was newly appointed, and she wasn't sure what to expect. Then she turned and acknowledged the prosecutor, Joel Smyth, a U.S. Attorney.

Joel returned her greeting. "Morning, Ms. Carey." He looked up at the judge. "Your Honor, may we approach?"

The judge nodded.

"Judge, there is certain information that has just come to light," said Smyth. "Before we proceed any further, may we retire to your chambers for a conference, off the record?"

The judge agreed, and the three proceeded back to his chambers. As soon as they were gathered there, Joel began. "Mary Ellen," he said, "we've had some developments in this case. Our witness, Monica LaBretti, is willing to testify that your client volunteered to get parts for her car. He apparently also said that he had contacts who could fix her up with any kind of car she needed."

"Your Honor," Mary Ellen said, "are we referring to the young woman sitting back there in the courtroom?" When he nodded, she continued. "My client admits to knowing her, but he has a much different account of what went on between them. But before I even get into any of that, I'm going to need an adjournment because I was not informed of her existence until—"

Joe Smyth interrupted. "Mary Ellen, believe me when I tell you that we've got hard evidence against your client. Please listen to what I have to say before you respond," he added as she tried to object. "You may find my proposal attractive. I certainly would if I were in your shoes."

She shut her mouth and sat back in her chair. Joe had been with the U.S. Attorney's office since he graduated from law school twenty years ago. He had that look of permanent exhaustion that seemed to come with the job, along with the paunch, the baggy blue suits, and the black scuffed shoes. But she knew from experience and reputation that he was an honest man who would be fair.

"We'd like to make a deal. You may not be aware, but Port Elizabeth has become, for the last several years, one of the country's major centers for exporting stolen goods. One of the main commodities in this smuggling operation is auto parts. By themselves or reassembled, they command a high price on the black market overseas, particularly in developing countries. We've had a task force investigating this operation for some time. Just recently we had a major breakthrough when we learned the identities of some young men, including your client, who have been acting as middle men for local chop shops and car thieves and international smugglers." He paused to make sure she was following him. When she nodded, he continued.

"The bar where they hang out was infiltrated, and one of

the agents made contact with your client. She's ready to testify that he was bragging about the international exporting business he was in and then offered to obtain any stolen parts that she needed. But," he said, ignoring Mary Ellen's attempt to protest, "we're after bigger fish and willing to make a deal. Just convince your client to reveal his contacts."

This must be what Fitz had been alluding to. He must be involved with this task force. How was David going to react to their offer? If he took it, would the case be over? Was it possible she'd have her children by the weekend? She was afraid to hope. But, she reminded herself, she was here for David. Right now she needed to concentrate on that. "My client says he's innocent, but I'll be glad to go back to him and discuss your proposal," she said. "I don't know how he'll respond."

"If he fingers his contact, we're prepared to consider a much lighter sentence," Smyth said. "Maybe even without jail time."

"That's it?" She could not believe that this nightmare could be over so easily.

"That's right," said Smyth as the judge nodded. "Off the record," he said, pausing to make sure he had her full attention, "we don't think your client would have the, uh, the gray matter to carry out the kind of operation we're talking about. This is big time."

What he said made sense, but she didn't directly respond for fear of compromising David.

"You'd do well to remind him," said the judge, "about the kind of sentence he's facing. If the U.S. Attorney can back up his story, he can demand a stiff sentence, and I have the power to comply. It could mean he'd be away for a long time. The young man doesn't look like the sort who would do well with jail. See what you can do to make him cooperate."

She nodded, hoping David and his father would listen to reason.

*   *   *

Mary Ellen joined the Andersons at the coffee shop across the street from the courthouse. It was typical of the area: crowded, noisy, poorly ventilated, but served good, reasonably priced food. It was filled with court personnel and attorneys, both government and private. She nodded to a few acquaintances on her way to the Andersons' corner table. She'd suggested meeting here because she wanted to get away from the courtroom and Monica LaBretti. She hoped that David would calm down and listen to reason once Monica wasn't a distraction.

The moment Mary Ellen sat down, even before she explained what had happened in the judge's chambers, Lois Anderson started in. "You have got to take care of my poor David," she said in her unnaturally high, babylike voice. "You know my David wouldn't do anything that was against the law." She turned to her son and started to smooth back his hair.

David swatted her hand away. "Ah, Mom, leave me alone."

Mary Ellen watched the exchange with resignation. When it came to Mrs. Anderson, the woman was so delusional about her baby boy that Mary Ellen had to be particularly careful about not seeming even slightly optimistic. Lois Anderson interpreted any sign of hope as meaning that David would get off without even a tap on the wrist. Mary Ellen had learned that the hard way.

Kirk Anderson impatiently interrupted. "So what's the story? What kind of a deal are they offering? That's what was going on back there, right?"

Mary Ellen nodded. She was determined not to let the man bully her. She figured he wasn't going to like what was being offered, but everything about the case told her that it was the best chance David had. It was obvious that David had done what they were accusing him of, and they apparently had the evidence to prove it. The only thing that made sense was for David to make a deal and tell the U.S. Attorney what he knew. David's father should be able to see that.

When the waitress left to get their drinks, she started to explain about the smuggling operation that was under investigation and David's alleged involvement. When she finished, she was met by silence. Lois Anderson sat, her jaw slack, but even she had to see that they were dealing with a serious matter, more than a schoolboy's prank. Kirk Anderson, on the other hand, looked angry enough to explode. After a few moments, David finally spoke, but to his father, not Mary Ellen.

"Does this mean I'm in big trouble? You never said that was going to happen!"

Mary Ellen interrupted. "We don't have to decide anything now," she said quickly. "Just let me explain the deal they offered, before you decide what you want to do."

Kirk Anderson was the biggest problem. She had hoped that he would be practical and understand that going along with the deal was the only way. But while she explained what the government was offering David in exchange for testifying, he continued to be silent. When they'd finished eating and were getting ready to pay the check, Kirk took her aside.

"I've tried not to put too much pressure on you," he said, a new hardness in his voice. "But you're giving me no choice. Get David off," he ordered. "Do whatever it takes, even if it means putting some money in the right places. But," and he pointed his finger at her for emphasis, "David is not going to talk to anyone about anything. Am I making myself clear?"

She nodded, trying not to let him see how frightened she was, afraid to imagine why it was so important to him that David not talk. Was it just concern that David was more involved than the prosecutor thought? She didn't think so. Even Kirk Anderson must realize that his son wasn't capable of anything more than following simple orders. Any other reason for his wanting David to stay silent was too chilling to contemplate—but she knew she would have to face it. And he actually suggested she offer a bribe to get his son off. The implications of Kirk Anderson not being honest was something she did not want to deal with. Her whole firm was tied up with him. What would be her future if she helped bring him down? The answer was obvious. Job-wise, she would have none.

Could it be that the Andersons just didn't understand the deal that the U.S. Attorney was offering? She needed to make a final effort to convince Kirk and David that the proposal was a lifesaver. If that didn't work, she had to get hold of Dunphy and tell him what was going on. Dunphy would not be pleased if she confronted Kirk without telling him first. But one thing was obvious. If she couldn't talk David into testifying, she had to get off this case.

She looked at Kirk Anderson and spoke firmly. "They claim they've got hard evidence against David. Assuming they do, he'd be much better off cutting a deal, and this one couldn't be better."

"No way," he said, shaking his head. "David's not a stool pigeon."

Chapter Nineteen

She walked the few blocks from the courthouse back to the office. The Andersons had offered her a ride, but she told them she needed the exercise. In fact, she needed to get away from them and be able to think. Why was Mr. Anderson so determined to get David off? She couldn't believe it was just because he was his son or because of the problem that Dunphy had mentioned about the building permits. There was more to it. It didn't make sense that a man would jeopardize everything he worked for so his son didn't look like a snitch and he could put up a building. If Florham Park wouldn't allow it, then why couldn't he put the building somewhere else? If he was found bribing a judge, he'd lose everything.

When she entered her office, the phone rang. It was Fitz.

"I like the way that short navy dress shows off your butt," he said.

How did he know what she was wearing? "Where are you?"

"Are you always so oblivious to what's going on around you?" he asked.

"What do you mean?"

"Just now, as you were coming back from the courthouse, I drove right behind you and you didn't notice."

She hadn't even seen him! Was she always in her own little world? She couldn't afford to be now, that was for sure. If she didn't see him, what else did she miss? She forced herself to laugh. "I was thinking," she explained. "I have a lot on my mind." If her phone was tapped, she didn't want anyone to think she was encouraging Fitz. Not after what had happened with Minky.

She'd missed him, but she was afraid to have anything to do with him until this case was over. She wasn't even sure if she should be talking to him on the phone. What if these guys were tapping it? With all they seemed to know about her, that had to be what was going on. But she needed to tell him about the cat. He had to know to what lengths these guys would go to frighten her.

"I'm sorry," he said when she told him. "I knew something was up when I saw you out there this morning, but I didn't want to take a chance and stop by in case someone was watching. I told you these guys are brutal."

"I can see that," she said in a rush. "And I'm scared. I don't even think I should be talking to you on the phone."

"Let me make that my problem. Yours is to focus on David's case so you can be back with your children," said Fitz. "Just keep an eye out. I may be behind you."

She wished he could be with her. She put down the phone with regret. He was right. She needed to focus on David's defense.

The phone rang again. This time it was Kirk Anderson. "I hope you didn't misunderstand me this morning," he said.

"Of course not. You're worried about your son," she said, cautiously. "I don't blame you." She didn't trust him, but until she knew what was really going on, she needed to treat him as she always had. "It looks like the best deal for David, but if you and he don't like what the prosecutor's proposing, then you don't have to agree to it."

"Exactly. But that's not why I called. I wanted to know if you're still getting those threatening phone calls. I spoke to David's friends, and if it's one of them who's been doing it, I am sure they'll knock it off."

Mary Ellen didn't think one of David's friends would have killed Minky. "I doubt it's one of his friends."

"What do you mean?"

She told him about Minky.

"What makes you think the caller was responsible?"

"He told me. He called later to say he'd do the same thing to my kids if I didn't do what he wanted."

"I can't believe it! What kind of people are they?" he said. "I'm very sorry it's turned out this way. Representing David is probably more than you bargained for." He paused, as if thinking about what he was going to say next. "You tell any-one about what happened?"

"I haven't had a chance to. I was thinking about calling the police, but to be honest, I'm afraid to." It wasn't exactly the truth, but close enough.

"Good thinking. I wouldn't. No telling what these guys will do next. You're better off keeping it to yourself and figuring out how to get David off."

After hanging up, she felt very much alone, particularly when she thought about her job also being on the line. She'd al-ready tried reaching Dunphy in Ireland when she got back from court. His secretary said he had probably moved on to their next vacation stop and had turned off his cell.

"He promised he'd call in sometime this week. When he does, I'll tell him you need to speak to him," she had explained after sighing heavily and giving Mary Ellen a look that said she was being a bother.

Besides, removing herself no longer seemed to be a realistic option. Fitz and his people needed her here to find out who was behind the phone calls, and more importantly, the smuggling in the ports. All her instincts told her that she was hot on that trail. Kirk Anderson looked like a good suspect.

Which meant that she had to figure a way to get David to come clean and at least tell her who he was involved with. That way she could work something out with Fitz and the Feds and make a deal with the prosecutor. They'd let David off and she'd at least be able to get her children back.

She called David's apartment. Fortunately, he was in. "We need to meet," she said. "I've been thinking about that deal the U.S. Attorney is offering."

"My dad said I couldn't do that. I can't talk to anyone."

"I understand that. But I must tell you, as your attorney, the deal they are offering may be the best you can do. If Monica testifies against you, which seems to be the plan, then you're probably going to be convicted."

"I don't want to talk about it. My dad said I don't have to talk to you."

"I don't have to be your attorney either. If you or he think you can get better counsel elsewhere—"

"I don't know about that. I just know he said you'd get me off and I wouldn't have to tell anyone anything. He said you'd fix it."

Interesting that his father would be so sure that she could fix it. "We should meet, David. As your lawyer, I need to know everything that happened. Then you and I can decide what to do next. If you don't tell me what's going on, you're making it very hard to figure out how best to help you."

"But my dad said not to talk to you." He was sounding less sure of himself.

"I'm sure he didn't mean that you couldn't have a conversation with me. He's probably just concerned that you're going to incriminate yourself."

"Huh?"

"You know, say something that might make you look guilty. Of course," she added hastily, "you aren't. But if you don't talk to me at all, I can't do my job. I can't present your case unless I know your story ." Mary Ellen hoped she didn't sound like she was pleading. "Why don't we meet for a burger? We can talk about what's been going on and if you feel comfortable about it, you can tell me what happened."

"You paying?"

"Sure, and you can even pick the place."

They agreed to meet the next day for lunch in West Orange at Pals Cabin. It wasn't far from David's apartment. Hopeful that she'd made some progress, Mary Ellen hung up and went back to the work in front of her. She needed to prepare motion papers to find out what kind of evidence the government had against David. If he came clean, she might not need them, but she couldn't count on his complete cooperation.

Minutes later, before she had a chance to settle down and concentrate, the phone rang. It was David.

"Maybe Pals is too close," he said when she picked up. "I was thinking we should go somewhere no one knows us. Okay?"

"I guess so. Do you have a another place in mind?"

"Yeah. Down in Elizabeth, just below the airport. There's a burger joint that's pretty good and we'll have some privacy. I'll be able to talk," he sputtered.

She wondered why he was so nervous. She was his attorney, there was nothing unusual about their having lunch together. Elizabeth wasn't terribly convenient, but David sounded so uneasy, she didn't protest. At least she would finally get to talk to him.

She went home that night tired and discouraged. When she unlocked the door and let herself inside, she was greeted by the two remaining cats. Their presence reminded her of the evil she was up against.

Without the kids, the house was too quiet. The only sounds were her footsteps or the cats playing in the rooms overhead.

The silence was shattered by the phone ringing.

She answered it and when there was no response except a dial tone, she carefully replaced the receiver, trying to ignore the beginnings of panic. It was probably a wrong number; that happened all the time. Or it could be a telemarketer. That too happened often, especially at dinnertime, which it happened to be. But tonight, when she felt like such a perfect target for whoever had killed Minky and threatened her and her children, any call made her nervous.

She would not let it get to her. She was determined to go about her routines as if nothing was wrong, to even prepare dinner. She decided to make herself a tuna fish sandwich and for once missed Minky's immediate response to the sound of a can opener. The sandwich was a failure. After a few bites, she realized she had no appetite. She wrapped up what was left and put it in the fridge. Then she gathered up the cats and the daily paper and went up to her air-conditioned bedroom. She had a phone there and the panel for the alarm. She'd lock her bedroom door, set the alarm, and get through the night.

At about nine o'clock she showered, put on her nightgown, and climbed into bed. She had a new mystery that she'd almost gotten into when she thought she heard something outside. With the air-conditioning on it was hard to hear anything, but she thought she'd heard a noise, possibly footsteps. She tried to put it out of her mind, figuring it was her active imagination, until she heard it again, this time the distinct sound of footsteps across the slate patio. When she heard a crash, it was impossible to pretend there was nothing going on. She picked up the phone and called the police. Then she grabbed the poker that was by the fireplace in her room, slipped on her robe, and tiptoed downstairs. She would just check it out before the cops came.

The kitchen was dark. She had turned out all the lights before she went upstairs. There was no moon. She couldn't see anything when she peered out the back door window. But she kept staring out into the darkness. She needed to know what was out there, and she was afraid to turn on the spotlight. Once her eyes adjusted to the blackness, she saw a figure in the shadows staring back at her.

Chapter Twenty

Without the moon, it was so dark that Fitz had to practically feel his way through the backyard—carefully, so he didn't step on the flowers and vegetables she grew. He remembered the garden, but he forgot about the furniture. He was still smarting from bumping into the dark wrought-iron lawn furniture that was, at night, practically invisible. Then she shut off all the lights in the house, making it even harder for him to find his way to her back door.

Not for the first time he asked himself if he was crazy taking a chance like this. He still couldn't come up with a rational reason why he was there. He just knew he had to see her. He couldn't let her be alone again tonight. He knew she desperately missed her children. When she told him about the cat, although she was calm in her telling, it was obvious that she was afraid. He needed to be with her. He could no longer fool himself. She had become important to him and he wanted her to know. That is, if he could make it to her back door without getting shot, or worse. He didn't think she had a gun, but when he saw her peering out the back window, it made his heart stop and his breath run cold. If she did shoot at him, she'd be in her rights and he would have only himself to blame. God help a lovesick puppy. He'd better get a grip before he put them both in danger. But first he needed to see her and make sure she was all right. He couldn't go another night without checking on that.

Already it was too late. Someone was on the back porch. Then she heard the doorknob rattle. She raised the fireplace poker with both hands and squeezed her eyes shut, prepared to crush the intruder's skull.

"Mary Ellen? Put that thing down before you hurt some-one, and let me in," Fitz whispered.

Her eyes flew open at the sound of his voice. "What are you doing here? Is something wrong?" Her heart was beating so fast, she could hardly catch her breath, much less speak. Her hands were shaking so badly, it was almost impossible to de-activate the alarm or unlock the back door.

"I'm sorry," he said when she finally managed to get the door opened. He hugged her to him as he spoke. "I just came to check on you. I didn't mean to scare you."

She clung to him, not wanting to let him go. Everything about him, including his outdoorsy, clean scent, was a reminder of how much she missed him. Hard as it had been to be alone until now, she knew it was going to be even harder when he left.

He rubbed her back with his powerful hands and nuzzled his chin against the top of her head.

"How are you holding up?" he asked.

She shook her head, glad that the darkness hid the tears that were starting to form. "I'd be okay if it weren't for the children," she said.

He pulled her closer. "At least you know that they're safe. I know you just wish you were with them."

"All I want is for it to be over," she said. "I don't know who to trust, and I don't even have Mr. Dunphy to talk to."

"What do you mean?"

"Oh, just that he's out of the office right now. He's somewhere in Europe so I can't even call him. There's no one in the office I can go to."

"It should break soon," he said.

She hoped he was right.

They continued standing in the darkness in each other's arms. She didn't want to let him go. It felt so good to be pressed against his worn polo shirt, enveloped by his powerful arms. It seemed like the only comfort she'd had in days. She looked up and saw that he was staring down at her, a half smile on his face.

When their eyes met, he bent down, found her mouth, and began to slowly kiss her. "You don't know how I've thought about doing this," he murmured before deepening his kiss. She returned it and welcomed him by reaching up and wrapping her arms around him to pull him nearer.

He suddenly stopped his kisses and placed his hands on either side of her waist. "We should get down, out of sight, just in case," he whispered, at the same time as he eased her onto the kitchen floor, until they were kneeling, facing each other. "We don't want to take a chance on anyone seeing us," he murmured into her ear.

She nodded, no longer as afraid. With him by her side, her fears were overpowered by her need to touch him and hold him. She wanted to run her hands through his thick soft curls, down the sides of his face.

When they finally separated. Fitz sighed. "I needed to see you and hold you and make sure you were all right. I hate that you're alone like this. You must be afraid."

She nodded in the darkness. "A little bit."

"I don't like that you're alone," he repeated. "Especially after what happened to Minky. How about if I camp out down here?"

"What about your boys?"

"I sent them to a neighbor's. They understood. They didn't want you to be alone either."

"Oh, thank you." She could feel the tears coming. "Thank them! I would feel better knowing you were here." She took a deep breath. "I'll be fine on my own tomorrow and the rest of the time. But tonight, after Minky—" Her voice trailed off. "I just would feel better." She went upstairs, fumbling in the dark, still afraid to turn on the lights, and got a blanket and a pillow. When she came back down and had made up the couch, she turned and reached for him. "Thank you for everything."

"Huh?"

"For understanding," she said, "that I'd be afraid and not want to be alone tonight."

He pulled her to him. "You don't have to thank me. I want to be with you. You've become very important to me—even my boys can see that."

He kissed her long and hard and then let her go. "When all of this is over," he said, "we're going to do something about us." He smiled at her and looked at her questioningly. "What do you think about that?" he said, taking her face in his two hands and looking into her eyes barely visible in the moonlit room.

"Sounds good to me," she said, smiling.

"Good! Now go on upstairs before I give in to temptation."

She did as he asked and was asleep within minutes, knowing he was downstairs protecting her.

When she awoke at six the following morning, for an instant she thought she might have only dreamed Fitz's visit. Then she rolled over and saw the note he'd left on the pillow.

She picked it up and held it unopened, hesitating, suddenly afraid of what he had written. But at least it was evidence that he'd been in the house. She opened up the folded piece of paper and read his message.

Dear Mary Ellen,

I had to come over last night. But we can't risk danger again, so we'd better not meet until this is over. I am always watching you, and if you need to reach me, call me at my central number in Newark and leave a message. Someone will get it to me.

Take care, my love. Now that I've found you, I don't want to lose you.

Fitz

Chapter Twenty-one

Mary Ellen was uneasy. From the minute she'd stepped out of the elevator into the garage underneath her office building, she'd felt as if someone was there. It was noon and the garage was empty, except for the attendant in his booth counting money. She wondered if she was being paranoid. She hoped Fitz was watching out for her as he'd promised. But she couldn't shake the feeling that danger was lurking. Why hadn't she told him about her lunch plans with David so she could be sure he was following her? She'd been so excited to see him last night that she hadn't thought of it. She prayed he was somewhere nearby as she buckled her seat belt and headed out of the garage to Elizabeth to meet David.

She turned down McCarter Highway. She would take it to Route 1/9, past the airport, to Port Elizabeth. At the first light, she checked her rearview mirror and made a mental picture of the cars behind her. Four blocks later she looked again. Three of the cars were the same. She forked to the left onto Route 1/9 and noted that there was only one car, a dark blue Honda, still there. Was that a coincidence? She tried to make out the driver, but it was three cars back. She couldn't even tell if it was a man or a woman.

When she got to Elizabeth and the Honda was still behind her, she knew someone was following her. Determined not to panic, Mary Ellen pulled off the highway and made several quick turns as she tried to lose the Honda. After four right turns and a detour into an alley, she wasn't sure where she was, but the Honda was gone. Cautiously, she retraced her path and found her way back to the block David had named.

He was waiting for her in the restaurant, seated in the last booth. She greeted him, sat down, and when she saw that he was nervous, opened the menu.

"So what'll it be, David? Bacon cheeseburger deluxe?"

"I'm not really hungry."

She looked up in surprise. He really must be a wreck to be off his feed. "Shall we talk first?"

He shook his head. "I can't tell you anything. I'll be in worse trouble than I already am. Please just leave me alone," he said, sounding as if he was going to cry. "Couldn't you have just gotten me off," he whined, "like Dad said you would? No one said I had to do anything."

"David—"

He stood up abruptly, before she could finish. "I'm getting out of here, before I get into any more trouble."

She stared at him for a moment, stunned by his performance. Then, when she saw that he was serious, she also got up. Quickly she walked through the restaurant, but not so quickly that she didn't notice a bald man at one of the front tables turn around, stare at her, and then call for the check. She briefly wondered if he might be watching her too. When she got outside and saw no sign of David, she forgot about the bald guy. How could David disappear so quickly? She scanned the blocks as she hurried to her car, mindful now that the bald man was right behind her. She picked up her pace, and he did too.

One thing was certain. She needed to call Fitz. She quickened her steps until she was running, understanding that David had set her up. Why else would he have asked her to meet him in such a desolate place?

She got into the car and locked the doors as she started the engine. She looked in her rearview mirror and noted that the bald-headed customer also got into his car, a black late-model BMW. When he pulled up alongside her, she braced herself. She had to stay calm if she was going to get out of here.

As she swung out of the space and pressed down on the gas, she fumbled in her purse for her cell phone. She had to keep moving, but she also had to get hold of Fitz. Even as she drove, quickly rounding each corner, she realized she was getting lost. But she couldn't stop driving.

After the third quick turn, there was no one in her rearview mirror. Grateful for the break, even if temporary, she punched in the number Fitz had given her for emergencies. She was still waiting for an answer when she made the next turn down a one-way street, away from the water and, she hoped, in the direction of Route 1/9. She nearly crashed headlong into the BMW parked sideways across the narrow street. She dropped the phone, slammed on the brakes, and quickly shifted into reverse, preparing to press down on the accelerator. But when she checked her rearview mirror, she saw the Honda from the highway right behind her, blocking her exit.

She was trapped. With cars lining both sides of the street, the road was too narrow for her to get by. She leaned over and grabbed the phone from the floor, pressed redial, and waited impatiently for someone to answer.

By now the two men were out of their cars, walking toward

her. She forced herself to stay calm. There had to be a way out. If she could just get through to Fitz. The phone rang several times, then finally someone picked up.

"This is Mary Ellen Carey," she said as she craned her neck to see the street signs. "I'm in Elizabeth, on the corner of Third and Geneva. Please tell Captain Fitzpatrick I'm here, and in trouble. Please!"

"Excuse me?" said the woman who answered. "Could you please spell your name?"

By now the men were standing at her car trying to open the door. When they discovered it was locked, the bald guy ran back to his car. The other guy, who was younger and built like a bull, started to lean on the car, rocking it.

"Please," she screamed into the phone. "Tell Fitz I need help. Right now!"

The phone went dead. Frantically, she pushed redial again, ignoring the two men outside the car. The younger one was now leering at her through the window and the bald guy was swaggering back with a crowbar.

She couldn't get the phone to work. It kept making short rings and then going dead. She tossed the phone onto the seat and tried to think, doing her best to ignore the two men who were both peering in at her menacingly.

The narrow street was lined with warehouses. Although the street was deserted, there had to be somebody who belonged to all the cars that were parked. She scoured the street looking for what might be an occupied building or a storefront. Half a block down she saw a open convenience store.

She studied her two adversaries. The bald guy looked to be about forty-five and was overweight. It was the younger one that she had to worry about. She knew she would have a hard time getting past them both. But she didn't have a choice. She looked in the backseat for something heavy to throw and saw a pair of Timmy's cleats and one of the law books from the office. She grabbed everything as she flung open the car door, knocking the younger guy off balance. She tossed the cleats in his direction and threw the heavy law book at the older one, taking them both by surprise. Setting her sights on the narrow alley just ahead, she rushed past them.

It was her two-inch heels that defeated her. Just as she started to make headway, one caught in grating in the alley. She stumbled and fell. They were on top of her before she had a chance to right herself and continue. When she turned to face them she saw that the older man had pulled out a gun. He motioned for her to get up.

They roughly pulled her to her feet. "Tie her hands behind her back before she tries anything," the older man growled.

Her whole body froze in terror when she recognized his voice. Her caller, the guy with the Jersey accent, the one who'd threatened her kids and had probably killed Minky. The younger man forcefully tied a rope around her wrists, but she hardly felt the pain. She was too frightened of what might happen next and knew that she had no way to call for help.

But she did her best to mask her feelings as she stared at the short, balding man and tried to figure out what to do. All she could tell for sure was that he seemed to be in charge of the younger man, who was less sure of himself. At least he was not the one holding the gun.

The bald one turned to Mary Ellen. "Gimme your car keys," he said, reaching around her back and grabbing them out of her clenched fist. She wished her house key wasn't on the same chain and realized that things couldn't get much worse.

He nodded to the younger guy and pointed to her car. "Park Ms. Carey's car and mine over on a side street while I keep an eye on her. Someone can come back later for them."

"Don't even think about trying anything," he said, turning

back to her. "Believe me when I tell you I won't hesitate to use this." He waved the gun in the air before swinging it in her direction. "I've been thinking about you, lady, for the last month," he added with a leer, in a tone that made her skin crawl.

Thoughts of her three children passed through her mind as he roughly pushed her in the direction of the remaining car. What would happen to them if she was killed? The prospect was unthinkable. She had to survive. There was no way these two losers were going to make her children motherless.

Mary Ellen sat in the backseat of the car behind the two men and assessed her situation. What could she do with her hands tied behind her back and a gun at her head? Stay cool, she decided, until she saw an opportunity to act. But she still feared for her life. She could hardly breathe, and her mouth tasted vile. She was having a hard time coming up with a workable plan. Against two men, one with a gun, with her hands tied behind her back, there wasn't much she could do unless she figured out a way to outwit them. She desperately hoped that Fitz had gotten her message and was on his way.

"He's not gonna be happy with us," said the younger guy to his partner.

"Because of her?" The bald one shook his head. "He won't be happy until she's out of his life."

Those words were a cold reminder of reality to Mary Ellen. She was on her own and fighting for her life.

She looked out the car window. They were heading down to the waterfront. She needed to calm down enough to assess the situation. If she tried to escape, there was nowhere to go. They wouldn't hesitate to shoot her.

When they pulled up to Kirk Anderson's main warehouse down on the waterfront, she wasn't surprised. It made complete sense that he would be behind all this. She desperately hoped that Fitz had already figured that out. Anderson's involvement wasn't good news. He wouldn't want her to know who he really was. He probably would figure he'd have no choice but to kill her before she told Fitz.

They drove around to the back of the large cinder block building and parked. The driver got out, opened the back door, and reached in and grabbed Mary Ellen. He tried to drag her out by one arm, but she automatically resisted. Going into that building seemed a lot more dangerous than staying where she was.

It was useless to fight. With her hands tied, they could easily overpower her, even without the gun. "I'll get out," she said with dignity, "if you let go of me and help me up."

"Just don't try anything," said the bald one. "You really don't want to keep the big guy waiting." He walked a pace behind her as she followed the younger man to the back door of the warehouse. She was sure his gun was pointed at her back.

After the bright afternoon sun, the inside of the warehouse was cool, dark, and forbidding. She could barely make out what was in front of her, and was afraid she was going to trip over something. With her hands tied, she wouldn't be able to break her fall.

The two men sandwiched her between them, quickly moved her to the staircase, and practically carried her up the short flight to the second floor. Because they were pressed against her she could feel a sudden increase in tension as they approached the second level. Their obvious fear did nothing to ease her own.

With her heart pounding and her hands sweating, she allowed them to push her ahead of them through a door into the reception area. Another door opened, revealing the man himself.

Chapter Twenty-two

As she tried to adjust to the sudden light, Kirk Anderson welcomed her as if her visit were an everyday occurrence. "Come right in," he said, pointing to the door of his inner office. "You're just the person I wanted to see." Although his eyes were cold, he smiled broadly as he led her into his private domain. "Wait outside," he barked at the two hoods. "I'll call you if I need anything."

When they were alone, he stared at her for what seemed like forever, with eyes as cold as diamonds, the broad smile still there, mocking.

"I imagine you want me to loosen that," he said dryly, pointing to her wrists. She nodded, not bothering to return his smile.

He ignored her hostility and took a pair of heavy-duty scissors out of his desk drawer. He carefully cut through the thick hemp. "I hope they were not too rough with you. Sometimes," he said indicating the cut rope, "they get nervous."

He didn't wait for a reply, but instead walked behind his desk and replaced the scissors in the desk drawer. Then he motioned for her to sit in one of the chairs across from him as he took a seat in the chair behind his desk.

"Surprised?" he said. When she didn't respond, he answered his own question. "I suppose not, considering you saw David earlier. But you didn't know before that, did you?"

She shook her head. Somehow it seemed important that she hadn't known before.

He rolled his chair up closer to the desk and leaned his chin on his upraised fingers. "We have much to discuss."

She nodded, aware that he was studying her closely. She wasn't sure what to say. She figured she should take a cue and act as if it was the most natural thing in the world to be brought here at gunpoint with her hands tied behind her back. Maybe it would buy her some time, enough for Fitz to find her before Anderson did her in.

"We have a proposal for you. One that I hope will be to your liking." He got up and walked around the desk over to a small refrigerator. "Can I get you something cold to drink? I'm just going to get some ice water but you're welcome to anything we have: soda, juice, a beer?"

She shook her head. He was enjoying this. She glanced around the room, looking for a means of escape. There were no other doors and the two windows probably were no help, being two stories off the ground. She wasn't sure if she had the nerve to jump that far.

Maybe she'd take him on directly. He didn't have a gun—at least not in view. He was big, but he was at least fifteen years older than she was, and wasn't in the best shape. If she grabbed something heavy, could she overpower him? Or would he push the intercom button and have his goons on top of her before she had a chance?

He poured himself a glass of water and, instead of returning to his desk, sat down in the chair next to hers. It was all she could do to keep herself from moving away when he leaned closer. She could see the perspiration on his upper lip, the pockmarks on his chin, and the wrinkles on his brow that she'd never noticed before.

He took a long sip and then put his glass down on a coaster on his desk before he finally spoke. "Let's start by talking business."

She nodded, relieved that he was finally going to get to the point. "You know that we ship containers of goods from the port here in Elizabeth to ports throughout Europe. We import goods from them in return. Did you ever wonder what exactly we exported?" he asked.

She hesitated before nodding. What did he want her to say? It was only natural that she had wondered. To say otherwise sounded foolish.

"I am sure you are aware that Eastern Europe is still behind us in technology."

She nodded again, her mouth too dry to speak.

"I was stationed in Germany when I was in the army thirty years ago," he said. "While I was there, I discovered there was a high demand for our consumer goods, particularly automobiles. The ultimate luxury for an Eastern European was an American car. But most American companies didn't bother with the Eastern European market. The common wisdom was that it would not be profitable. Understandable, since no one over there had any cash. However, I observed that there were always people with money, and that those who had money had an unquenchable thirst for American goods."

She was beginning to understand. "You mean the black market."

He smiled. "Exactly. Even then, as an enlisted man in the army, I knew an opportunity when I saw it."

"So you've been stealing cars here, filing off their serial numbers, and shipping them over there?"

He beamed at her as if she were his star student. "I knew

you were quick. And because we get rid of the VIN numbers, sometimes even dismantle the cars, no one has been able to trace them. In fact, we've never had a problem!

"I have been in business for more than twenty-five years. But not until now have I ever had to worry about my opera-tion. Now suddenly Fitzpatrick, his friends in Customs, and even the FBI are breathing down my neck. I am in danger of losing everything. I can't have that happen."

She nodded, pretending to look concerned. She understood from how much he was telling her, and the way he was look-ing at her, that he wanted something. It was probably the only reason she was still alive. "So it was you that—" she started to say, but he interrupted her impatiently, his mood seeming to change.

"I'll get to all your concerns. I'll be the one setting the agenda. For now, let's just say that I've brought you here because I have a proposal for you."

She forced herself to nod and settled back to listen.

"It's common knowledge that you're divorced," he said, the conversation taking an unexpected turn. "I understand that your ex-husband is starting a new family. He is slow with support payments and sometimes doesn't pay at all. When that happens you are completely dependent on what you make at the law firm, and with your expenses that isn't always enough."

She tried not to show how unnerved she was as he laid out all her intimate financial secrets. She told herself that most of the information was easy enough to get. It could have even come from Dunphy in normal conversation. But then Ander-son listed how many times she'd been late on her mortgage and credit card payments.

"You make a decent salary at Dunphy & Boylan," he said, continuing to stare at her with that penetrating gaze. "But we know why you can't always pay your bills, don't we?"

She nodded in dismay.

He rubbed his hands together and almost chortled, appearing to be enjoying himself. "Yes, I am aware of your ex-husband's spending habits and the kind of loans you assumed as part of the divorce agreement."

She shook her head, unable to speak.

"I was impressed that you refused to sell the house and disrupt your children's lives. That would have been the easiest way to pay it all off. But I may have a way out for you. Are you interested?"

She didn't answer.

"Before you turn me down," he said, putting his hand up as if to caution or silence her, "I think you should pay attention to what I have to say. What if I told you that I know where your children are?"

"What do you mean? How could you? Even I don't know that."

She couldn't bear the smirk on his face.

"You'd be surprised what I know. Let's just say for argument's sake that I've always known, but until now haven't acted on it. I've had other things on my mind."

She nearly screamed out in anger. How could he know where they were? But although her stomach was churning and her head was pounding in rage and frustration, she forced herself to stay still. She did not want to give him the satisfaction of watching her suffer as she realized that her children weren't safe anywhere—not even in the "safe house" supplied by Fitz's people.

"I don't believe you," she said, hoping she sounded credible. There was, of course, the chance that he was bluffing, but she couldn't risk that.

He shrugged. "We have our sources and ways to get information. You and I need to come to a meeting of the minds if you want your children to be safe—if you want to live as you wish. Actually—just to live."

"What do you want?" she asked, hoping that her voice belied her true feelings. This man was pure evil. But she couldn't lose her cool.

He smiled and took a sip of water before he continued. "What I want from you is something very simple, and in your best interest."

He paused again to take another sip of water. She tried to muffle her impatience, wishing he would just get on with whatever it was that he wanted.

"My business has been running very smoothly until now, when your friends have become very interested in what we do. Lately they have been making a nuisance of themselves. The last straw was when they arrested David. You and I know it will never stick. He screws up small projects. No one in his right mind would think he could run anything as complicated as this operation. He just doesn't have the stuff—a magnificent disappointment," he said, laughing harshly. "And where I am most vulnerable," he added softly, almost as if he were speaking to himself.

He shook his head impatiently, as if he was trying to shake off whatever thoughts he had on the subject of his son.

"I won't let them get me like that. If David's arrest has made my business untenable, at least at this location, I'll go somewhere else.

"That's where you come in," he said, nodding to her.

She looked up questioningly.

He explained. "I want you to join our organization, and help me with my new location."

"Excuse me?"

He nodded, almost beaming. "I want you to be our general counsel."

"No," she said quickly. "I couldn't possibly."

He pressed his index finger on his mouth and shook his

head. "I was hoping for more enthusiasm, but happy or not, you have no choice."

He was right. She didn't have the luxury of saying no. She would hear him out. It would buy her some time. "I am curious about your offer," she said, "although I don't think I'm really what you're looking for. But maybe you can tell me more?"

"I can understand your hesitation," he said. "Listen carefully and think about the alternatives.

"In many respects you are already working for me, so it really isn't a big change. I've had the opportunity to see you in action and to see what a good lawyer you are. I have also come to see something more important. Your loyalty—even to the likes of David, who"—he met her eyes and nodded—"we both know is foolish and weak. Maybe his mother and I spoiled him. In any case, he would not be in my organization if he weren't my son. But you?" He slowly inspected her, as if she were a prize specimen. "You could go far. And as a woman . . ." He paused and shrugged his shoulders. "Perhaps having a female lawyer is one of my more brilliant ideas. A woman in such a position is more sympathetic. I want you to work for me. To represent us here in the U.S."

Mary Ellen's mind was spinning. Anderson was offering her an opportunity to save herself. If she could make him believe that she was going along with what he was proposing, it would, at least, buy her time and maybe a chance to escape. "And if I say no?"

"I am prepared to offer you a very attractive package."

She nodded, but kept quiet when he suggested $500,000 as a base salary for the first year. That was more than she would make in five at Dunphy & Boylan. Combined with the bonuses that he indicated would be a regular part of her package, it was enough to set her up for life and to guarantee her and her children everything they could possibly want.

"And of course," he added in conclusion, "you would move away from Maplewood—away from your former associates and friends, like that cop and the lawyers in your office. You'd start a new life, in a place where your children would go to private schools, and where you would be close to our new base of operations."

"Where would that be?"

He hesitated at first, as if considering whether to trust her with that last bit of information. But then with a shrug, he continued. "I've already set up a business in Miami. You might want to consider Coral Gables, one of Miami's more affluent suburbs. Are you familiar with the area?"

She nodded. "I was there once on business. It's beautiful." She paused to consider how to respond. "I have to admit your offer is tempting. My children would like the weather and, of course, having the water so close. That would be nice. But what makes you think you will be immune from the law down there?"

"Because you will take care of me," he said, smiling. "You are going to make sure that the police and customs and anyone else never bother me again."

She shook her head. "Even if I could do that, what would make me want to?"

"Your children's safety."

Her breath caught in her throat. "What do you mean?"

"When we are down in Miami, no one would ever suspect you of being a smuggler or a thief." He stood up, as if it was all settled, and reached for the phone. "We will begin right now. You will call your friend at the U.S. Attorney's office and convince him that David has nothing to offer them so they drop the case against him."

She shook her head. "There's nothing I could say that would convince them of that. Besides, how will that help you?

Even if they drop the charges against David, they will figure out a way to get you."

He beamed. "Maybe, maybe not. But by the time they draw up the papers for me, I'll be out of the country and you'll be in Miami ready to show them that we are legit."

"But they already suspect you."

"They don't have any proof. That's why they've gone after David. They must have figured that would be the easiest way to get hard evidence against me. But all it's done is show me that they don't have anything solid. I'll be gone before they find anything."

"And me?"

He smiled. "You will have relocated to a friendlier climate."

"You've got it all planned. But they'll catch you."

"No, they won't." He beamed. "I've been working on it for some time. About a year ago, when I sensed there was an investigation brewing, I started a legitimate import-export company down in the Port of Miami. If and when I am ready to resume this highly lucrative operation, everything will be in place."

Chapter Twenty-three

Mary Ellen knew she would have to sound convincing when she made the call, or she'd be finished. She thought back to her senior seminar in trial techniques and about what Professor Silverman had said the first day: *Good litigators usually have a touch of the actor in them. That's why they can successfully represent views they don't agree with. Someday,* he said, *it will be your job to convince the judge and jury that you and your client are of one mind, whether or not that's true.*

"So if I understand you," she said, looking Anderson square in the eye, "if I agree, you want me to call the U.S. Attorney's office and convince them to drop the case against David."

"Exactly. That's your test."

"That's not going to be easy," she said, stalling. Of course there was no way that he would agree. Anderson wasn't stupid, but he seemed to think that law enforcement worked the same way as his experience in business, that people could be easily manipulated. That was her answer, she supposed. Make Anderson believe that she could manipulate John.

"If I tell my friend at the U.S. Attorney's office that I have new information," she said, looking at Anderson with what she hoped was sincerity, "he might go for it. I'll tell him that David is ready to make a deal."

She considered what might sound somewhat realistic and believable to him. "I'll tell him that in return for dropping the charges, David will give him some hard evidence on other illegal activities in the port."

"I don't want David telling them anything."

She nodded. "He won't. It's just the first step of the bargaining. My thought is that we'll string them along, maybe with a few hints here and there. It won't be until you are safely out of the country that they will realize we haven't given them anything worthwhile. The worst-case scenario at that point will be to plead guilty to a lesser charge. David might have to pay a fine. Or he could join you wherever you are."

"That will give me time to clean out these warehouses and get everything out of here."

She nodded. "Exactly."

"It might work. Only way we'll know is if you make the call, so do it," he said abruptly.

She realized that her palms were soaked as she reached over and picked up the receiver. It was only willpower that kept her fingers from shaking as she dialed the number for the direct line to Fitz. He might not be there, but she was afraid to call the switchboard again after what had happened the last time. It was going to take some acting, and it didn't help that the man she had to perform for was sitting so close she could practically feel his breath on her neck. But it was her only chance.

Fitz answered, her first lucky break. "John," she said, speaking quickly, "you're going to want to hear about the deal I've got for you."

"Mary Ellen? Where are you? I'm frantic. What's going on?"

"Yes, exactly," she continued. "It's about David Anderson's case. In fact, I'm sitting right now in Anderson's office at his warehouse in Elizabeth and we've come up with a proposal."

At that moment the door to the reception area flew open and the two thugs rushed in. The bald one grabbed the receiver out of Mary Ellen's hand. "She double-crossed you, Boss. That call was to her cop friend. We heard him answer on the other end."

The younger man grabbed Mary Ellen and forced her arms behind her back. He pulled a length of rope from his pocket and bound her wrists together, even tighter than before.

Things were happening so fast that she could hardly think. But not so fast that she didn't have time to look over at Anderson.

He caught the look and snarled. "You know I've no choice but to have you killed," he said, staring at her with those cold, heartless eyes. The tone of his voice convinced her that she was as good as dead.

Anderson turned to his men. "Take her to the container yard across from the piers and get rid of her."

She knew it was over when he didn't even glance at her as the two men dragged her out the door. "Don't prolong it," he added. "I know that's what you'd like to do, but in this instance, I'd rather you didn't."

Tony nodded as if it were business as usual before he pushed her out the door and shoved her down the stairs. "Get a move on," he snarled. "I gotta make a few phone calls and change my plans. I didn't expect to be busy tonight."

They got into a car and didn't have to go far before they reached a fenced-in yard, with what looked like miles of shipping containers. Her mind froze in terror when she realized what was happening. If they put her in one of them, no one would ever find her, even if Fitz knew to come down to the yard.

The younger man put the car in park and turned off the ignition.

"Open the container before I get her out of the car," said Tony. "I don't want to give her a chance to try anything."

While the younger man did as he was told, Tony pulled her out of the backseat and shoved her toward the container.

Mary Ellen pretended to stumble. If she got him off balance, maybe she could make a run for it. But Tony pulled her up before she had a chance. He stuck his gun in her back, reminding her of what he wouldn't hesitate to do. To make matters worse, when she stumbled, she'd lost one of her shoes. She tried to turn back for it, but Tony made her take the other one off too and, taking it from her, tossed it over his shoulder into the darkness.

The gravel hurt her feet, but Tony wouldn't let her slow down. "It's your own fault you don't have your shoes. Besides, you're not going to need them where you're going."

Together the two men dragged her over to the open door of the container, picked her up, and threw her inside, slamming the door behind her. When they threw her in, she lost her balance and fell to the floor, scraping her face against the rough wood of one of the pallets.

She did her best to ignore the pain and the stickiness that she knew was from fresh blood and tried to roll over so she could sit up. She needed to concentrate on saving herself. It wasn't easy to sit up without the help of her hands, but eventually she managed by locking her feet under one of the pallets, using her legs for leverage. She heard a lock being attached to the container door, and her heart sank. She wondered how much time she had before they came back for her. Although it seemed hopeless, she knew she had to try to get help. She sat motionless, almost not breathing, and listened for any sounds. She wanted to make sure the two men were gone. She heard the engine start and the sounds of a car pulling away, then nothing but silence. She sat a few minutes more until she was sure no one was outside. Then she shimmied over to the side of the container to look for something sharp to cut the rope wrapped around her wrists. The splintered edge of the pallet she had fallen on seemed the best choice. She rubbed the rope back and forth across the edges for what seemed like forever and was about to give up when the rope finally started to fray. After some more rubbing, she'd worn the edges enough to allow her to pull apart the rest.

Elated at her small victory, she suddenly felt as if she might really make it. With newfound determination she began pounding on the container's aluminum wall. When that didn't seem loud enough, she started screaming.

Minutes later she heard the lock of the container click and then the sound of the door creaking open. "What do you think you're doing?" shouted Tony. He pushed his way in and grabbed her by the arm. "Get more rope from the car," he called out to his buddy. "We'll gag her and tie her to one of these pallets. That way she won't be able to get into any more trouble."

Chapter Twenty-four

Mary Ellen threw herself against Tony. Taking him by surprise, she succeeded in knocking him over. While he lay sprawled across the floor recovering, she lurched toward the container door. She knew that once the younger man arrived, it would be over.

Instead of going down the plank in front of the container, she jumped the two feet to the ground, momentarily forgetting she was shoeless. She ignored the pain that shot through her as she hit the pavement. She could hear Tony shouting from behind her, "Catch her, you idiot!"

"Stop, before I shoot!" It was Tony's partner. She kept running, hoping that if he did fire the gun, he'd be a lousy shot or she would be far enough away. Just as she turned down one of the rows of containers, she heard the gun go off. From the clanging of metal, it sounded as if the bullet ricocheted off several containers, but it didn't hit her. She ran on, turning again, down another row of containers and then another.

It was just about dark and she was having difficulty making things out in the yard. She was tired and out of breath. Her feet hurt, and with the sun down, she was cold. She reminded herself that so far she'd managed to get away from them. But it was not over. They were the ones with the gun.

"You're not going to be able to escape!" Tony shouted into the darkness. "There's two of us and one of you. You know we're going to find you. You're not going to get very far."

She was just on the other side of the container from him. If he turned around and saw her, she'd be dead as soon as he pulled the trigger. She pushed away the mounting panic. Tony was losing patience. If she kept her cool, he'd be the one to make a mistake. All she had to do was wait, out of sight, until someone else came into the yard. Then she would get help.

But how long would that be? She stood pressed against a container, close to where she last heard Tony's voice. For what seemed like hours, there was nothing. Suddenly she sensed someone close, so close she could hear him breathing.

She had to stay calm, quiet her pounding heart. Just because he was close didn't mean he knew where she was.

"Thought you were going to get away with it, didn't you," Tony said softly, his voice piercing the darkness. He was right next to her. She felt the cold steel of the gun press against her neck and froze in terror. Her heart was in her throat as she waited for his next move. Would it be her last?

Tony grabbed her arm and kept the gun pressed against her head. "I've got her!" he shouted.

It was then that she became aware of a figure standing in the dark directly across from her, behind Tony.

Even in the darkness she could tell that Fitz's gun was drawn, aimed straight at Tony. But Tony's gun was aimed at her. If she could distract Tony for even a second, Fitz might be able to overpower him.

Tony was muttering something about his partner's incompetence. This was her chance, her only one. She turned as if to look at him, falling against him as she did. In the process, she knocked his gun, not out of his hands, but at least away from her. Instantly, Fitz was on top of him. She got out of their way and Fitz grabbed the gun from Tony's hand and wrestled him to the ground. When he threw the gun out of Tony's reach, she scrambled over and reached for it just as floodlights hit the area. At the same time, she heard the sound of a gunshot and the voices of other men. Everything was happening so fast she could not keep track. All she understood was that she was not going to die.

But it wasn't over. Fitz and Tony were still struggling, and she cringed every time Tony lashed out at Fitz. She gingerly gripped the gun. She had never held one before and hoped she wouldn't have to use it. But if it was to save Fitz or herself, she was ready. Abruptly Fitz turned with a grunt, and with a sudden motion, swung at Tony with his right arm while he undercut with his left, finally knocking him out.

For a moment Fitz stood there, breathing hard, looking down at Tony, who had crumpled to the ground. Then he grabbed him by his jacket and dragged him over to one of the cops who had just arrived. "Cuff this guy," he grunted, "before he comes to." He turned to one of the other cops. "Somebody taking care of his buddy?" The cop nodded, pointing to two men who were leading the younger man over, his hands behind his back.

Mary Ellen rushed over to Fitz. His face was bruised and she knew he was hurt. At the same time, waves of relief washed over her. Could it finally be over? After the hours she had just spent, she couldn't believe it was she, not the two hoods, who was the victor.

"You okay?" Fitz asked as he reached out and pulled her close to him.

It felt so good to be safe beside him. "Fitz, my kids— Anderson said he knew where they were. Has anyone been in touch with them? Is there some way you can check and make sure they're okay?"

Fitz nodded. "I'm sure he was bluffing, but I'll have someone get right on it." He let go of her and hurried over to one of the men standing nearby. Fitz said something to him and the man went over to the police car.

Fitz returned to her side. "He's going to find out right now," he said. "In the meantime, we're going to have to bring these guys down to the precinct to be booked. I'm afraid you'll have to give a statement. Can you handle that?" he asked, looking at her with concern.

"Of course," she said. Word that her children were safe, followed by a hot bath and bed, was all she wanted, but she knew she had to do her part to finish this up.

"I won't leave your side," he said.

She nodded gratefully. The traumas of the day seemed to be finally getting to her, and she wondered how much longer she could cope.

The policeman sent to check about her children came back. "Your children are fine," he said. She felt such waves of relief. Until that moment, worry had been a heavy cloud hanging over her.

"I told them what Anderson said," he explained to Fitz. "They are going to move the children again tonight."

Mary Ellen was about to ask when they were coming home when Fitz turned away to tell the other cop to take the two prisoners on ahead. She and Fitz would follow in his car. She watched as the police cars pulled out, their lights flashing.

When the cars were gone and they were left in the near darkness, Fitz's demeanor instantly changed from businesslike to affectionate and concerned. His eyes locked with hers as he reached out and folded her in his arms, crushing her against him. "Oh, Mary Ellen," he said, so softly she almost didn't hear him. "I was so scared I wouldn't get there in time. I thought I was going to lose you." He relaxed his hold just enough to see her face, and looked at her closely. "Are you okay?" he whispered. "Did they hurt you?"

She shook her head and pulled him even closer as she buried her face in his chest. She could not speak. "I'm fine," she finally managed. "Now that you're here. You were just in time."

He continued to hold her, his strong arms tight yet gentle as he caressed her back. Finally, with a sigh, he released her. "We've got to get down to the station house and get this over with. Then I can take you home. Okay?" The last question was said almost shyly.

She looked up at him and nodded, still overwhelmed.

It wasn't until they started to walk to his unmarked sedan that he noticed she was shoeless and limping. "You lost your shoes," he said.

She started to explain when he reached over to pick her up. She began to object, but he ignored her protests, scooped her up, and cradled her against his chest. Gratefully, she conceded. When they reached the car, Fitz opened the door and gently placed her on the front seat, where she settled with a deep sigh.

"If you hadn't gotten here when you did, I'd probably be dead," she said as he got into the driver's seat. "You haven't told me what happened to Anderson," she said. "Did you pick him up?"

He shook his head. "By the time we got to his warehouse he was gone. That's where we went first," he explained, "after we got your call. There were fire trucks on the scene when we arrived. It looks like most of the contents of the building were destroyed, but we left a few guys there to sift through the remains."

"How did you know to go to the pier and search the container yard?"

"It seemed like the obvious place, once we knew you weren't at the warehouse. We were just lucky we found you. If you'd been locked in one of the containers, we never would have."

"I know," she said, explaining how she had escaped. Fitz's only response was to sigh and reach down and clasp her hand.

"But what about Anderson?" she pressed.

"We're looking for him," he said. "The guy is smart. He may have gotten away, at least for the time being."

She told him about Anderson's offer and his plans to leave the country.

"Can he get away with that?" she asked.

"There are certain countries that will harbor a fugitive."

"But what about his family? He wouldn't leave them here."

Fitz turned off Route 1/9 onto Raymond Boulevard, and headed into Newark, where the station house was located. "He didn't."

"He didn't what?"

"Anderson didn't leave his wife and David. He moved them. At least that's what we think. They're gone. Vanished."

"David skipped bail?"

"Apparently. Some of my men checked his apartment and his roommate said he left late this afternoon for the airport." They'd reached the station house and parked the car. "We've got agents watching all the airports. I'm optimistic that it's only a matter of time until we find them."

She forced herself to ask the question that weighed most heavily on her mind, the answer to which she was the most afraid to hear. "Do I have to wait until you do before I get my children back?"

He'd come around to her side of the car and bent down to lift her out, but he paused at her question and frowned. "I don't know." He continued. "I wish it were that simple, but unfortunately, since we don't know where Anderson is, we don't know if your children will be safe if we bring them back here. I think we need to wait a bit longer."

She didn't like his answer, but she knew he was right.

With Fitz's help, it didn't take her long to identify the two men in a lineup and give a statement. When they were done, Fitz took her home to Maplewood. As they drove through the local streets to her house, Fitz cleared his throat a few times, seeming to have something to say. Her mood was subdued, knowing that she would once again arrive home to an empty house and that her babies were far away. Fitz pulled into her driveway, cut the engine, and turned to her.

"Let's get you inside," he said, reaching for the door. "I bet you're ready for that hot bath. You've had a rough day."

He came around to her side of the car, opened the door, picked her up, and carried her up to the house.

"You should put me down," she muttered, embarrassed to be carried in front of her own house. What would the neighbors think?

He shook his head and continued to hold her. "It makes no sense for you to walk until we get your feet taken care of."

He was right. She could rationalize his carrying her. It made sense. But when they reached her front door, they had another problem. She didn't have her keys. Anderson's men had taken them to pick up her car.

He squinted at his watch in the dark and shook his head. "It's late," he said. "Too late to call a neighbor. You don't have an extra key hidden in the yard?"

She shook her head. By now he'd put her down and the two sat side by side on the front steps of her house.

"We have two choices," he said.

She looked at him, just barely making out his expression by the glow of the streetlight, and waited expectantly. She was too tired to deal with anything. She would have to rely on him to solve any problems they'd encounter tonight.

His solution wasn't what she expected. "I can break in," he said. "It's that or put you up in a hotel. Your choice."

"I want my own bed, my own tub." For some reason she couldn't bear the thought of a cold, antiseptic hotel room. She wanted, she needed, to be home.

Fitz didn't seem surprised at her preference. "Then we have

our answer." He stood up and leaned down to pick her up. "Let's go around to the back door and get this over with."

If she'd been expecting something sophisticated, she would have been disappointed. Fitz did exactly what Mary Ellen would have done if she'd been alone. He used a rock to break a windowpane on the back door, put his hand through the opening, and undid the lock, setting off the alarm as he did.

"How about a glass of wine?" he asked after they were inside and had disengaged the alarm and checked that the cats were alive and well.

She nodded, pointing to the refrigerator. She gingerly walked over to the cabinet and got two glasses.

"Can I get you anything else?" she offered, handing a glass to Fitz.

He shook his head. "Maybe later. Right now I just want to get you into that bath."

It did not take any convincing for him to carry her upstairs to her room, where he gently laid her on her bed.

Again she found that she was happy to let him be in charge. In fact, she felt as if she were in a trance, incapable of any decisions. It was all she could do to lie back against the pillows and watch him as he opened the wine and poured two glasses.

He handed her one. "It looks like even you have reached your limit," he observed.

She nodded. Speaking was beyond her.

He went into the bathroom and came back carrying a wet washcloth, a small bowl of water, and some antiseptic. He put them on the table next to the bed and sat down beside her and started to wash her bruised feet.

"You're a tough cookie," he said as he reached over, lifted up one foot, and looked closely at it. "Doesn't look too bad. You've got some cuts that I want to clean out, but nothing too deep."

His touch was gentle, and even when it hurt as he carefully

washed and then prodded each foot to check for hidden glass or debris, she did not mind. Not when it was Fitz.

It felt so good to feel his firm yet gentle touch, after all that had happened. It also was obvious from the way Fitz tended to her that she was the only thing he cared about at the moment.

After cleaning her cuts, he stood up, went back into her bathroom, and turned on the water to fill the tub. "Do you want me to put some bubbles in?" he asked, coming back into the room holding two bottles of scented suds.

She shook her head. "It'll only sting," she said.

He nodded. "I'll leave you to your bath," he said. "I'll be in the next room if you need me."

"Thanks for staying tonight," she said. "After all that's happened, I don't think I could manage by myself."

"That's what I figured." He walked over to the side of the bed and bent down to kiss her. "Sleep tight. I promise you that tonight you are safe."

She nodded and watched him walk out of the room, shutting the door behind him.

Later, as she lay in the tub and tried to let go of the day's accumulated stress, she thought about Fitz. What was it about this man that stirred up such desire and yet brought out such love and affection? The depth of her feelings and passion were new to her and made her feel vulnerable. She knew she was already in over her head and only hoped that he was right there with her. Later, when she was finally in bed and about to drift off to sleep, she understood that even though she had only known Fitz for a short time, she had fallen in love. She hoped that he had feelings for her in return.

Chapter Twenty-five

The sound of the phone knocked her out of her dreamy sleep. Who could be calling at this hour?

Mary Ellen bolted upright.

Fitz called from the next room. "Do you want me to take that?"

"No, I'll get it."

She ran to the phone, her feet still tender, and managed to pick up the receiver before it went to voice mail. When she held the receiver to her ear and greeted the caller, there was an ominous silence. She wondered if she had missed the call, and then a man spoke. "Ms. Carey, you listening?"

She nodded, her hands automatically tightening on the receiver. "Yes, I'm here."

"It's not over. We have unfinished business."

Her throat seemed to close and her air supply vanished. She took a deep breath and tried to speak. "What do you mean?"

Fitz was instantly beside her. "Who is it?" he mouthed.

She shook her head. She didn't know.

Fitz indicated he was going downstairs to pick up the phone

in the kitchen. Her job was to keep this guy on the phone. But she was in a state of panic, and her mind froze.

"Your kids are still in danger."

"What do you mean?" she croaked. It was as if someone had put a vise around her head and twisted it tight. Did they know where her children were? "What do you want?"

"One thing: Anderson's safety. Keep your people away from him. Don't interfere. He gets away and we'll leave your kids alone."

Before she could answer, there was a dial tone and then an expletive followed by a long frustrated sigh of exasperation. Fitz must have been on the line. "They obviously spotted our guys."

He ran upstairs, where he found her sitting in her rocker. Arms crossed, head down, she rocked back and forth while she tried to sort out what was happening and what she should do.

He grabbed a blanket from the bed and wrapped it around her, pulling her close to him as he did. "I know you're worried about them," he said. He crouched down and took her hands in his. "I don't think they can find them. We have good people taking care of them. Anderson's people are trying to frighten you."

She forced herself to look up and meet his eyes. She didn't understand any of it. Fitz told her he'd keep her children safe, and yet every time she turned around, somebody was threatening them. Why hadn't they caught Anderson? All of these people were searching for them and yet she was still receiving these calls. Her first inclination was to look for her children herself and make sure they were safe. But she knew that was not the answer.

"You have to find Anderson!" She searched his face.

Fitz nodded. "We have information that he was seen at the airport in Newark and then again in Miami. Unfortunately, he's smart and disappeared before we could arrest him."

"Why didn't you tell me that before?" she said. What else was he holding back, and why? Didn't he trust her, or did he think she couldn't handle it? Her children were being threatened. Wasn't she entitled to know?

As he pulled on his shoes and socks, Fitz explained. "I didn't want to upset you, especially after what you had gone through. I thought you'd had enough for one day."

She tried not to be angry. Who asked him to protect her? Didn't he respect her enough to treat her as an equal? "So what happens next?"

"We keep watching the airports and other points of exit and continue looking back here to see if he left any clues as to where he was going."

She nodded. "He said he's set up a place offshore that he's been preparing for months."

"That was useful for us to know. Now we just have to figure out where."

"Probably some island in the Caribbean."

"There are a lot of islands. It might take some time." He cleared his throat. "I've got a few phone calls to make and then I should go down to headquarters. We will step up the search. Will you be all right?"

She nodded. "Of course, but there must be something I can do."

He shook his head. "It would be better if you just sit tight and stay safe." He sighed and lowered his voice as he looked over at her earnestly. "Then I won't be worried about you. I don't want you to take any more risks."

"But my family is in danger! My children," she said with emphasis. "I'm not going to just sit back and wait to see what happens. I need to help!"

"These guys are pros. They won't stop at anything."

That was why she needed to be involved.

She waved him off as he got into the car, barely able to contain her frustration and anger. As she watched Fitz pull out of the driveway she thought about what she would do. Even if he didn't like it, she wasn't going to stand on the sidelines and wait for him to fix things. She had been on her own too long to do that.

She wasn't able to fall back to sleep, so she was one of the first to arrive in the office. She was determined to talk to Dunphy. He was an old friend of Anderson's and should be able to answer some of the questions she had about the man. Dunphy was due back from Europe, but if he wasn't back, she was going to insist on speaking to him.

That turned out not to be necessary. When she arrived, the receptionist told her Mr. Dunphy was in his office. As usual, when there was a crisis, his door was shut, but his secretary waved her through.

Dunphy stood up from his desk and came around to greet Mary Ellen when she entered. "I heard about what happened to you on the news as I was driving in this morning," he said, briefly hugging her. "I didn't expect you to be in today. Are you okay?"

She nodded. She was so relieved to have him back and in charge.

"I feel very responsible for what happened," he said after they both sat down. "If I hadn't insisted that you take this case, you wouldn't be in any kind of danger. And your children! What did you do about them?"

She sighed. "I don't know where they are, which almost makes it worse," she said, explaining about the safe house. "The police won't tell me so I won't inadvertently give it away. But it makes it very difficult."

He nodded sympathetically. "It must be terrible not to know."

She agreed.

"But won't they be coming home now that Anderson is out of the picture?" asked Dunphy.

"He's not out of the picture yet. And they're not coming back until he is."

"What if they don't find him?"

She sighed and shook her head. "That's what I'm afraid of. And I don't know how much longer I can take it."

He nodded with understanding. "It goes without saying that you can take as much time off as you need. All of us here want you to know that if there is anything we can do, don't hesitate to ask."

She nodded. "Thank you. I appreciate that, but actually, I think I will do better if I work."

He seemed to understand. "You have other cases in progress?"

"Plenty to keep me busy. All the cases I put on hold while I was defending David."

"Speaking of which, for obvious reasons, I want to put all of Anderson's files in my office until I figure out what to do with them."

She nodded. That made sense. They probably would be subpoenaed. "Did you have any idea what he was involved in?" she asked.

Dunphy looked up, seemingly startled by her question. "Of course not! What a suggestion!"

She nodded weakly, unnerved by his anger. She supposed it might be offensive to suggest that he knew what Anderson was up to, but his reaction took her by surprise.

Chapter Twenty-six

Before handing over the Anderson files, Mary Ellen pulled out David's folder. She wanted to go through it one more time. Maybe she had missed something. She might have been so involved in David's defense that she'd overlooked something important, something that would tell her where the Andersons were hiding.

It didn't take long to discover there were documents missing, namely all the responses she'd prepared to the government's interrogatories. She didn't remember them containing anything suspicious, but then again she didn't know then what she knew now. It was another hour before she was sure the documents were not in the file and had not simply been misfiled.

Fitz called in the middle of her search.

"Is it safe to talk?"

After her conversation with Dunphy, she wasn't so sure. Fitz said he was close by, so they agreed to meet at the diner across from her building.

"I don't want you working there," he said after they ordered.

She scowled. What he said made sense, but she didn't want to hear it. "Excuse me?"

"I don't want you exposed. You're too close."

She started to protest, but he interrupted. "Hear me out. I've been around long enough to know danger when it's there, and your office is infested."

The fact was, she had the same feeling. Something wasn't right. But every nerve in her body balked at being told what to do. Perhaps he sensed it, because he gave a deep sigh. "Even if I didn't feel about you the way I do, I would tell you to leave—that it's too dangerous for you to stay involved."

She didn't respond. She was too busy dealing with her conflicting emotions. The waitress came with their coffees and he waited until she had left before speaking. "I'm in love with you. I didn't expect it to happen, not so quickly, especially not on the job, but there it is, and there's not a thing I can do about it. I don't think there ever was," he said softly, almost to himself, as he reached across the table and took her hands in his. He looked deeply into her eyes. "I think I fell for you the first time I laid eyes on you, as silly—or romantic—as that sounds. Anyway," he said with a sigh, as if relieved to get the admission off his chest, "crime, or the detection of it, is my business. I know what I'm doing and if you have any respect for my judgment, you will listen when I tell you that you need to get out of that office. Something is going on and it won't be long before it blows up, and when it does, you are the natural target. You know too much."

She was unsure how to respond. He had just told her he loved her. She loved him too. He also was telling her what she didn't want to hear—that she had to back off and leave the job to him.

He looked down at her hands in his. "I just hope it isn't already too late. If Dunphy is involved—"

In spite of her own suspicions, suspicions she didn't want to believe, she reacted. "Dunphy? What makes you suspect him? He's like a father to me, or at least a mentor."

"I hope you're right," said Fitz. "I know you care about him. But there's something about this whole deal that doesn't add up. I think it's got to do with Dunphy. If I'm right, if he's in this with Anderson, he won't hesitate to hurt you."

She shook her head. "Isn't it better for you to have me there? If I leave, they'll think we're on to them. That could make it worse for my family."

"Your children are safe. That's confirmed. Now you have to think about yourself. You're no good to them if you're dead."

She grimaced. "You're being dramatic."

He let go of her hands, reached across the table, and touched her cheek. He shook his head. "I wish I was."

She took his hand and held it for a minute, wishing she could give in to what he wanted, but that was impossible. "Let me think about it. I understand what you're saying and I can see how it might be risky for me to be there. I'm just afraid that leaving will raise suspicions, or at the very least alert Dunphy— if he is involved. Lawyers don't do that. It's not professional. This is my career. Am I supposed to quit because you have a *feeling*?"

He groaned in frustration. "I understand that you are not used to having someone in your life who cares about you and maybe feels entitled to tell you what to do. But believe me, I wouldn't be saying this if I wasn't so sure that it's dangerous for you to be there."

"I have to be there. I need the money. Don't you understand that? I have a mortgage, just like you."

"You can find another job—in a place where your life isn't in jeopardy."

"I am touched by your concern," she said, not caring that

her sarcasm was evident. "It's not so easy to find another job." Abruptly she got up, leaving her coffee untouched. "I should get back to the office and get my work done."

She felt no satisfaction as she walked out of the restaurant. In fact, leaving Fitz was the last thing she wanted to do, and even as she did it, she had second thoughts. Was she being stupid, insisting on maintaining control? Was he right about Dunphy? What about her children? When would she see them again?

In spite of the fact that the man she loved had just told her that he loved her, she was miserable. It did no good to tell herself that she was better off without him or that they were obviously unsuited. That would be a lie. They'd been through enough together for her to know they were a perfect match. But right now, she must concentrate on discovering Dunphy's role in this Anderson mess, including finding those missing papers from David's file.

She was careful in her quest. She told no one, since she did not know who she could trust. When she had exhausted all the possibilities she could think of, including searching all the other files that she had worked on during the past month, she faced the fact that she would have to check Anderson's other files—the ones she had handed over to Dunphy. Maybe her papers had been misfiled in one of his other cases. Instead of asking Mr. Dunphy if he had seen them there, she stayed in her office, waiting until eight o'clock, when she was sure everyone was long gone.

She wasn't surprised to discover that Dunphy's office was locked. She might have done the same thing if she had custody of all of Anderson's papers. But she wasn't going to let a locked door stop her. The receptionist kept a master key in the event anyone locked him or herself out, and Mary Ellen knew exactly where it was kept.

About a half hour later, she got the key and unlocked the

door to Dunphy's office. Just then she heard the elevator door open and someone get off. She was tempted to shut out the lights and hide under Dunphy's desk. Instead, she quietly closed his door and stood stock-still in the middle of his office, waiting to see what happened next. She didn't even realize she'd been holding her breath until she heard the sound of a vacuum cleaner. *The cleaning service.* With a sigh she glanced at her watch, noting the time as 8:45. She set to work.

Although she was looking for part of David's file, it was impossible not to observe what was in Anderson's papers. Some of them were small litigations that she remembered from office talk. Others had to do with the formation of Anderson's corporations, including the company in Florida.

When she saw how that file contained such detailed information about the way the company was formed, she was forced to acknowledge that Dunphy knew too much about Anderson's affairs not to be part of it. Even if the corporation was legitimate, he had to have known something was going on.

The next file she went through had to do with Anderson's contracts with Polish exporters. They did not seem to contain anything that could be construed as illegal or involving the black market. Interestingly, though, the cargo Anderson imported to Poland was not specifically itemized, but simply referred to generally as "assorted goods." Had Dunphy ever asked what the goods were?

She still had a hard time believing Dunphy was knowingly involved in something illegal. He had so much to lose.

When she came to the next file in the stack, she knew she had come upon something important. The folder was simply marked *Anderson Misc.* She scanned each document with care. About halfway through the papers, she came upon the lease for property in Belize.

Startled, she sat down in the closest chair and read the document. From the brief description, it sounded as if this was not a place of business, but a residence, with several bedrooms, a kitchen, and a living room and dining room. It was dated six months earlier. That was about the time that Anderson said he had started making contingency plans. Had Dunphy been involved in the planning from the outset, or was he initially misled? What did it matter? He obviously knew now.

Why Belize? She tried to remember what she knew about the country and what might make it attractive to someone like Anderson.

The lease had to be important. She considered taking it home. But she didn't want Dunphy to realize it was missing. She decided to make a copy and get out of there.

By now it was 9:15. The cleaning staff was gone for the night, and she was alone. She went into the copy room, turned on the machine, and waited for it to warm up. Her mind raced from the nagging question of Belize to thoughts of Fitz. She shouldn't have been so defensive with him. But she was independent and not looking for anyone to take care of her, even if he had been right about Dunphy. Still, she had to talk to him and show him this lease. It just might lead him to Anderson and it certainly incriminated Dunphy.

She reached for the phone and called Fitz at home. She made it brief. He was clear about not wanting her alone in the office, but he sounded excited by what she had found. She promised to bring it over as soon as she had made a copy.

Just before she got off the phone, she heard the elevator doors open and a few voices. "Gotta go," she said. "I should be there in about half an hour." She tried to keep her panic out of her tone. The copy room was right next to the elevator. Whoever was there would see her when they got off.

One of the voices was Dunphy's. How had she left his office? Fine, except for the one file that she was now copying. Then she remembered. The lights were still on.

Footsteps were fast approaching. There was a second voice, one she did not recognize. She glanced around the room looking for somewhere to hide, but there were no dark cubbyholes or corners, and the florescent lights lit every crevice. She grabbed the original version of the lease and her photocopy and stuffed them into the file folder. She took a deep breath and tried to compose herself.

When the voices were close, she poked her head out of the copy room door. "Mr. Dunphy!" she said brightly. "What brings you out at this hour?"

He stopped speaking in midsentence. "Mary Ellen. What the blazes are you doing here?"

"Finishing up some work. In fact, I was just heading home," she said, forcing her voice to sound normal. She looked at Dunphy's companion, a small, olive-skinned man, and waited for an introduction, but none came. She turned back to the copier and turned it off, quickly gathered up her papers and the folder, and started toward the door.

"Hold on, Mary Ellen." There was a sharp edge to Dunphy's voice now.

"Excuse me? I was just about to leave. It's late," she added quickly when she realized that he wasn't going to step aside.

"What are you working on?"

She hesitated, wondering what to do. From the look on Dunphy's face it was clear he meant business. Did he know she was on to him? She couldn't let herself think that. She had to stay cool.

"I was just making copies for one of my files," she said, moving away from him and toward the door.

"Hand me the file. Don't make this more difficult than it has to be."

She did what he asked and then slowly turned to face him and the gun that his companion was holding.

"I didn't want to have to do this," Dunphy explained, "but

you couldn't leave things alone, could you?" He turned to the other man. "Go into my office and get what we came for. This shouldn't take a minute."

She watched as the man handed Dunphy the gun and left the room. She suddenly understood that he intended to kill her. Her mind went into overdrive, making it impossible to think rationally.

"I worked it all out," Dunphy said. "Made Anderson the fall guy. But then you had to stir things up, asking questions and not leaving well enough alone. I thought when the Andersons were gone and your kids were threatened you would have the sense to give it up. But the very next day you're in here snooping around. You give me no choice. I have always been fond of you, but I'm going to have to get rid of you. Otherwise, it's over for me."

How could she save herself? She forced herself to stay calm. She noticed that Dunphy wasn't comfortable holding the gun and wondered if he knew how to use it. She couldn't risk finding out, but maybe she could get it away from him.

"I never thought you were involved, even when I realized Anderson was," she said, stalling.

He smiled, as if pleased. He seemed to welcome the opportunity to explain himself. "I'm smart. I always covered my tracks. We never should have been discovered. But Anderson was stupid when it came to his kid, and we both know the kid didn't have the stuff. He fed right into the cops' hands." He shook his head. "I knew something like that would happen."

"But why you? You have a good practice. You don't need the money."

He shrugged. "You're right. It wasn't for the money. It was fun, and exciting. Practicing law, especially the kind we do, gets old after a while. Running the kind of operation Anderson and I had kept me young. I was always on the edge. There's nothing like the rush you get from living like that." She saw that he was so busy talking that he seemed to be forgetting what this was about. Although he continued to hold the gun, his grip had loosened as he talked, and he was even gesturing with the gun.

She shook her head to let him know how amazed she was by his brilliance and maintained eye contact, hoping he'd continue talking.

He did. "I know it's not for everybody, and my wife doesn't have a clue. She's like you. She wouldn't like living with the stress and excitement. But she sure has liked the comforts the business brought, and she never questioned why we could make several trips to Europe every year. But then she thinks, like most people, that lawyers make a lot of money." He nodded at Mary Ellen, who watched the gun as he pointed it away from her, but only for an instant. "You and I know that isn't quite the case." He sighed. "I wish I didn't have to do this. I wish you had accepted Anderson's offer." He smiled sadly at her. "That was my idea, by the way. You're a good lawyer and I've come to trust you. I would have liked to keep working with you."

He stopped speaking, straightened out the gun, and narrowed his eyes. She realized they were probably close to the end of the line. She had to do something. She was determined not to die here, not without a fight. She had to distract him.

"The original idea was Anderson's, right?"

Dunphy looked at her, startled and annoyed. She saw the gun slip slightly. She pressed. "He's the one that was in the army over in Germany. Right? He's the one who came up with the original scheme."

"No, never! Is that what he said?" Dunphy scowled and shook his head. "It was my idea from the start. He just helped me put it into action."

"He said he was the one who came up with the idea. He said you just helped by giving him the money to start the operation, but that he was really the brains behind it and the one in charge."

Dunphy's eyes bulged, and his whole body started to shake as his voice reached an eerie pitch. "That's a lie! Anderson is barely smarter than his son. I'm the only one with any brains, the one with the know-how."

She nodded as she watched him let the barrel of the gun point to the floor. With one quick thrust, she rushed toward him, and when he grabbed her with his free hand, she reached for a letter opener she'd spotted on a nearby desk. She thrust it firmly into the back of his hand that was holding the gun.

He screamed as he let go of the gun, and she kicked it across the room and started running. She barreled out of the room and down the hallway, determined to get past Dunphy's office and down the stairs before he or his friend had a chance to follow her. It was fifteen flights, but her heels were low and she could be fast when she needed to be. Still, she could hear the sounds of their approach as she flung herself down each flight.

In minutes she was in the parking garage, where she dashed for her car, grateful that she still had her purse. By now she was painfully out of breath, but continued running until she reached her car. Once inside the car, she started the engine and made her way to the exit while she frantically dialed the local police on her cell phone. The phone was still ringing when she saw Fitz's car pull into the garage, nearly crashing headlong into hers.

Chapter Twenty-six

Hours later, Mary Ellen and Fitz sat at a small square table in his kitchen, cups of steaming tea before them, his boys asleep upstairs. They were back from the precinct, where Dunphy was taken after being arrested and where she had told her story, including the new information about Belize. The cops said it would only be a matter of time before Anderson was arrested. The only snag was that Belize did not have an extradition agreement with the United States. "But we'll find a way around that," said Fitz. Dunphy's involvement was still sinking in. She had trouble believing Dunphy had been behind the whole thing—including the threats to her children. She turned to Fitz.

"Did you always suspect him?"

Fitz shook his head. "Only when he suddenly left for Ireland. It was too much of a coincidence. By the way, that fellow with Dunphy tonight was to be the new head of operations in Florida."

"You mean he already had plans to cut Anderson out of the business?"

Fitz nodded.

"As long as they catch them all," she said with a sigh, "and bring back my kids."

Fitz smiled. "They're on their way." He looked at his watch. "Their plane is due to land in forty-five minutes."

She leaped up from the table. "Then what am I sitting here for? When were you going to tell me?"

He grinned. "We've got time. Finish your tea and I'll drive you."

On the way to the airport, in spite of her excitement at seeing her children, she still had questions.

"What's going to happen to the firm? Dunphy was it. There is no one to replace him."

Fitz reached across the car seat and squeezed her hand. "You'll have no trouble finding another job."

He was right. She would look for a place where she could represent the good guys, for a change.

She looked out the window as they approached the airport. There was something else she needed to say while they were still alone.

"About today," she began.

He looked sheepish, seeming to read her mind. "It's my responsibility as a police officer to protect you from harm, but I know I was heavy-handed in my attempt to protect you. Just because I fell in love with you didn't give me the right to make decisions for you. I don't want to lose you," he said softly. "There has to be a way we can work this out."

She nodded. She had already come to the same conclusion. They could work out their differences. What convinced her of that was Fitz's look of pride when he credited Mary Ellen with outwitting Dunphy to the government officials that had been working with him. That look went a long way toward showing her that he respected her.

When they reached the airport and exited the car, Fitz

walked over to the passenger's side and took her hand. "Do you think you could be happy with me on a regular basis?"

She looked up at him, just barely making out his deep penetrating gaze. "What do you mean?"

He leaned down so that his forehead touched hers, sighed, and pulled her closer. "Will you give me a chance?"

"Give you a chance?"

"Will you get to know me now that this is over?" He paused. "You know, go on dates, stuff like that, to see if we're suited."

She looked at him questioningly. "I'm not sure . . ."

"I love you, Mary Ellen. I think you love me. We've established that. Now I just need to know about the rest of our lives together." He paused. "I think we've got a chance to make it."

Epilogue

One year later

They decided on a summer wedding at the beach, since that was where it had all started. Fitz's buddy down in North Carolina was delighted to lend them the house for the week—as long as he was invited to the wedding. Mary Ellen worried at first that their friends wouldn't want to travel all the way to North Carolina, but John Susino voiced what many of them seemed to be feeling: "The two of you together is a sight nobody would want to miss." There was going to be quite a crowd.

Mary Ellen saw even more of John now that she was working with him in the U.S. Attorney's office. She found that she was excited to be back doing criminal law and that it helped to have someone at home who had similar interests. Sometimes Fitz and she even worked on the same cases. The money wasn't as good as it had been at the firm, but fortunately, since she and Fitz had combined households by selling both of their